Exterminated Angel

Prose Series 17

Gérald Godin

Exterminated Angel

*Translated from the French
by Judith Cowan*

Guernica

Montreal, 1992

Original Title:
L'ange exterminé

Copyright © by Gérald Godin and Les éditions de l'Hexagone, 1990.
Translation © by Guernica Editions and Judith Cowan, 1992.
All rights reserved.

Antonio D'Alfonso, editor.
Guernica Editions Inc.
P.O. Box 633, Station N.D.G.
Montreal (Quebec), Canada H4A 3R1

This translation was done with the consultation, help and encouragement of Guy Godin.

The Publisher acknowledges financial support from The Canada Council and Le ministère des Affaires culturelles.

Legal Deposit – Third Quarter
The National Library of Canada and La Bibliothèque du Québec.

(Prose series; 17)
Translation of: L'ange exterminé.
ISBN 0-920717-68-3

Godin, Gérald, 1938-
I. Title. II. Title: Ange exterminé. English. III. Series.

PS8513.O347A8513 1992   C843'.54   C91-090585-1
PQ3919.2.G63A8513 1992

Chapter One

Polacks

Everyone at the paper bought his loose tobacco from Wolfrid Milton, a hugely fat man so obese that in the spring they would use him for testing the weigh-scales for the big trucks before the thaw.

He lived on the second floor and to get to the kitchen door of his place you had to climb the worn and rotting steps of a rickety outside staircase, then get past a scowling bulldog who seemed to be trying to bark himself to death, pausing after each volley of barks for a series of consumptive wheezes. As if to compensate, his mouth was all pink and blubbery, like an adult vagina. And once he was used to a customer, which took a few dozen visits, the barking would be replaced by an obligatory licking. But Wolfrid's tobacco was so good and so cheap that – fuck the dog – we went anyway, ready to face whatever was necessary to get our unbeatable roll-your-owns, which in those days we used to call *polacks*.

The dog's name was Kirkland and when he couldn't find a hand or a finger to lick, he'd always manage to find some other skin surface, such as a leg under the trouser-cuff, just above the sock. And then he'd let himself go completely, *le grand amour*, a wall-to-wall French kiss and, in your sock, the Flood.

Wolfrid Milton also had a brother named Racine, and when Racine visited Wolfrid, or vice versa, they would talk back and forth at the top of their lungs, as if they were a quarter mile apart, and in the middle of the sort of blizzard that would take the horns off a team of oxen.

Because they'd come into the world during a time when tuberculosis was skimming off all the prettiest children in the country and their mother, Dolorosa Milton, had decided that there was only one really efficacious remedy against the disease. Good lungs. And how to develop good lungs?

'Elementary,' said Dolorosa, 'those kids have to howl. They have to yell their heads off.'

So, she'd made sure that they acquired the habit, which they kept up for the rest of their lives.

A family that brays together stays together. They could be heard bellowing from the far end of the street and all over the neighbourhood. Sometimes the neighbours were worried.

'What's going on at the Miltons' place? Are they killing each other...?'

'No, nothing like that,' said anyone who knew them. 'They're practising preventive medicine....'

And, at such times, Kirkland, terrorized, would go and hide under the water heater, hunkered down on a fresh copy of *The Gazette*. It was just warm enough there and he could drool in peace over its fire-and-brimstone editorials.

Then the Milton brothers would then begin their mixing.

'This tobacco is for who, this morning?' Wolfrid would ask.

'Elliott's mix,' said Gerry Gretz.

And out from under the sink they'd drag a series of old round cans filled with very fine-cut tobacco from which they produced a blend that made the best roll-your-owns in the world. The colours of their tobaccos were fabulous. There was one that was blond, like the hair of the lovely Miche; there was one that had a touch of straw, like a freshly-mown hayfield; there was another that carried a hint of deer-meadow fawn; and there was one that was the transparent white of those few leaves that spend the winter on the tree and that roll up around themselves against the cold.

From all these blonds, golds and whites, Wolfrid and Racine could concoct a tobacco that would make you forget the bellowings, the barkings and the wheezes, Kirkland's slobber in your sock and the stairs that were dangerous even on the best days of summer – not to mention the worst days of the winter – as well as their pigheaded personalities and their working hours which put any normal human understanding to a rude test.

When Elliott's special was ready, Wolfrid would pinch it up in his fat, stiff fingers – like overstuffed piglets – and put it into a Kraft brown paper bag.

'Never in plastic, Monsieur Gretz. Always Kraft paper, from the Wayagamack mill. Because the brown paper breathes. Otherwise, in no time at all, the tobacco would be as dry as corn flakes and just not smokeable.'

All that for the polacks which Elliott would roll for himself during his long weekends, instead of simply planting his arse in front of the T.V. and watching sports programs. But he never offered any of it to anyone else. To have that right, you had to have worked at the paper for at least five years, get your stuff in on time, and give them a hand with type-setting on Saturday nights.

Then, as tastes evolved from tobacco to more stupifying drugs, Gretz was hardly stupified when one day Wolfrid Milton, instead of offering him his Elliott special, offered him Columbia Gold and the Sorel special, while awaiting delivery of the Marchessault or police station hash, cut with dried yak dung, coke, psilocybin and crack.

But this was a change dictated by fashion and it changed nothing at all. The ritual was the same in all its smallest details, and Kirkland still barked his head off, then calmed down, and started licking ankles. Until the day when Gerry

Gretz discovered that Wolfrid Milton had a little daughter and that they called her Gri-Gri, because of her grey eyes. And that now she was living in one of the condo towers on Peel Street.

Chapter Two

Rue du boc

Madame Bouillé's store offered a selection of all the candies in the world for one cent each. Hanging from the ceiling just over the door there was a bell which rang with a tinkly ding-a-ling every time a customer pushed the door open. Then the owner, who was none other than Dolorosa Milton, would rush out of the back room to stand behind her counter.

She said to Gerry, 'Know why I bought this place, Monsieur Gretz?'

'How could I? It must be one of your best kept secrets,' said Gretz.

'Well I'm going to tell you, *petit sacripan*. I bought it in memory of my father, Jean Narcisse, who for over a quarter century was the biggest one-cent candy merchant in all of eastern Québec and the inventor of the peppermint. On his tombstone there's a white marble peppermint to remind us all of his contribution to the world history of candy. There was a time when the Narcisse family had twelve trucks on the road, all over the country and all loaded with one-cent candies.'

Dolorosa's candy counter was her theatre and every shelf was like an Italian stage décor where, according to the seasons, the bonbons would change places. From generation to generation the neighbourhood children had come there to buy candy, pressing their middle fingers against the glass to make sure there would be no mistake: 'I want three of those, and two like that one, and one of the little three-cent syrup cones.' The glass pane along the bottom of the counter bore the fingerprints of three generations, a collection which would have put Bertillon himself to shame. On the cashier's side, the counter had two sliding doors for access and, depending upon the season, there were always some candies which moved up in rank and appeared on the counter.

'Those are my best sellers,' Dolorosa would say.

She also sold cigarettes for a penny. In those days they were Turrets or State Express, the best in the world for the simple reason that they're gone now, part of a vanished era, the time of childhood and the days when smoking was forbidden. Gretz had built a bird-house and had hidden it in the thickest part of the trees so he could use it to keep his packets of State Express Three-Three-Three and Turrets with their handsome little tower of grey stones against a red background.

The other service which Dolorosa offered to the children of the neighbourhood was buying back empty bottles.

'It teaches them about the capitalist system,' she would tell their parents. 'And it keeps them from cutting themselves on broken glass, too.'

Chapter Three

Gri-Gri Milton

The elevator refused to stop at the ninth floor and went all the way on up to the twenty-seventh before condescending to redescend to the ninth. The lighting inside it was piss yellow, the sort of yellow that made everyone riding the elevator look as if they'd just escaped from a submarine which had spent six months under the ice of the Arctic.

Studying himself in the mirror which made up the whole rear wall of the elevator, Gerry decided that he looked a bit like a Pirelli tire that had done the Indy 500 twice in a row. From the twentieth floor on down, under the disapproving eye of another passenger who glared at him all the way, he kept his finger firmly pressed to the button for the ninth. And the elevator stopped at the ninth floor. Number 914 was the last apartment at the end of the hall, on the left.

When he found himself alone in the corridor, Gerry opened his jacket and checked his underarms to make sure that his twenty-four-hour deodorant stick was still working. After that, reassured, he rang eleven short rings at the door of Miss Dragana 'Gri-Gri' Milton.

The eleven rings were to say, 'This is just the beginning and I shall fight on.' When he heard footsteps, he put his finger over the peephole as usual.

A soft voice asked, 'Who is it?'

'Gerry Gretz, reporter,' he replied – to his feature for the week.

The door opened. When he saw Gri-Gri, Gretz nearly fell out of his Wallabees. Skin as white as milk, hair as black as jet and wafting Miss Clairol shampoo at him, with eyes as grey as a Samoyed and slightly enlarged by a fine line of blue crayon. She was wearing nothing but a white terrycloth bathrobe, swiped from the Hôtel Meurice because it was decorated with a greyhound surrounded by a wreath of laurel leaves.

'Enter, do enter, Monsieur Gretz,' she said to him and he followed her into a sitting room which overlooked Côte-des-Neiges. The sunlight was so dazzling that Gretz had to shade his eyes with his hand in order not to trip over the futons which were laid out in a sort of a square around a low table made of imitation marble.

Gri-Gri sat down with her back to the sun and folded her legs modestly beneath her. But just as Gretz was about to ask his first question, she suddenly exclaimed, 'Monsieur, come here, Monsieur!'

Gretz felt something panting near his feet. It was a white poodle.

'Come here, Monsieur, come on, jump onto me!' said Gri-Gri, 'come and warm up my thighs, I'm freezing....'

As she unfolded her long legs, Gretz thought he caught a glimpse of the black fluff of her pubic hair. He wiped that image from his brain however and opened his notebook, Bic in hand.

'Tell me, Miss Milton, what are you called?'

'You've already said it, Miss Dragana Milton.'

'No, I mean in your job. Do you say pusheress or pushatrix or what?'

'Personally, I like pushette,' she said, 'like Little Miss Muffet, but pushier.'

The further he got with the interview, the more attracted Gerry felt to this young woman who was the only daughter of Wolfrid Milton.

He had a hard time concentrating on his questions. He was sure that all the remarks she was addressing to her dog were really messages intended for him.

Then suddenly she said, 'Anyway, Monsieur Gretz, even if I did like you in that way, you mustn't get any ideas, because I never go to bed the first time. And besides, I'm totally frigid. Whatever it is they mean when they talk about an orgasm, it's just a word to me.'

'But tell me, Miss Dragana, otherwise called Gri-Gri, why Monsieur?'

'You mean the name of my dog?'

'Yes.'

'Maybe I'll tell you one day, if we become friends.'

Gerry closed his orange notebook and politely asked where the telephone was.

'In the kitchen, Monsieur.'

Then Gerry telephoned the paper to tell them that he would be there on time and that everything was fine, talking loudly enough for her to hear him. When he stepped back into the sitting room, Miss Gri-Gri was completely naked and was delicately holding the nipple of her left breast between the thumb and index finger of her right hand – 'just like the painting by Jean Fouquet, in the Musée de Blois,' thought Gretz, trying to get control of his reactions.

'Don't act so innocent, my hero. This is just before my period, I'm horny and I'm kidnapping you.'

She got up, took him by the hand, and led him authoritatively towards her bedroom. She pulled the covers off the bed. Another futon.

As Gerry took off his clothes, he congratulated himself for having put on a nice fresh pair of navy blue underpants that very morning. And he was careful to lay his trousers out flat on the carpet, making sure that the creases were straight. He took off his watch and put it in his Wallabee so as not to forget it. But then he changed his mind and put it on the bedside table so as to be sure he would forget it.

At last he stretched out full length beside the very warm body of Miss Milton. She turned towards him and stared into his eyes.

'Why are your eyes so wide open?' she asked him.

'I've got such a hard-on that there's no skin left for my eyelids,' he told her.

Then they discovered that they were both impotent and went peacefully to sleep. When they awoke, Gretz asked her if he had hurt her.

'You've got to get out of here,' she said. 'I've got a delivery to make.'

As he put his shoes back on, Gerry discovered that Monsieur had eaten half of one of his Wallabees. He limped back to the newsroom.

'What happened to you, Gretz?' asked Baril.

'I caught my foot in the door of the Métro.'

'Yeah sure, at Milton Station,' said Elliott.

'Ah, go shit, boss,' said Gretz, with finality.

Chapter Four

The Seiko

'Message for you, Gerry. Urgent.'

The message couldn't have been clearer: *Found, old Seiko watch. To be returned to the owner's own hands only. From G.-G. Milton.* It was Gri-Gri, the little bitch. Very sweet, except that now the whole newsroom would know that Gretz had had an in-depth interview with her. You don't take off your watch to play dominoes. Well, that was just too bad. Let them say whatever they wanted.

From the car phone in his faithful Blandine, a Pontiac Parisienne that had braved the rigours of flood, snow and even hail, Gretz called Gri-Gri.

'I hear you have a priceless watch which needs to be picked up. When can I come and get it?'

'Don't you even say hello to your friends, you mannerless lout?'

'Didn't want to bother you. I know how taken up you are.'

'Taken. From time to time, yes, but unfortunately not by you.'

'Okay, enough fooling around. When can I see you?'

'You said see. Is that all you want? Depends what you mean by see.'

'I mean when are you visible?'

'Visible? So I was supposed to be invisible?'

'Pardon my French. I only meant that I want to come and take a look at you with my hands.'

'Hang on a minute,' said Gri-Gri. 'Do you really think that all you have to do is announce you're on your way for me to go into heat and start panting to make love to you? I'm not a robot-woman.'

'Okay, okay,' said Gerry. 'Anyway, it's not you I want, it's my Seiko. At least it performs.'

'Come over whenever you want, Gretz, but not before nine o'clock tonight because I've invited my boyfriend up for supper.'

So after the Canadiens had chalked up their seventh straight defeat, Gerry called his favourite waiter Ti-Mé over and paid for his four beers, his two sheep's tongues in vinegar, his bag of chips and his cheese curds. It was ten-thirty. The boyfriend must have lifted anchor by now and gone off home – probably with his erection still tucked under his arm.

Gerry imagined Gri-Gri tidying up, getting rid of all traces of the boyfriend, changing the sheets and making the bed, washing the dishes and, above all, throwing out the butts from his goddamned Celtiques.

Gretz had a nose like a fox. Even with the butts flushed down the toilet, the smell of Celtiques was clinging to the walls. The sheets, on the other hand, smelled too clean. She'd just changed them. It was clear that she'd invited the boyfriend into her bed, maybe as recently as half a hour ago.

'Explain one thing to me, you little bitch,' said Gerry to her. 'You kick your boyfriend out. The house still stinks from his Celtiques. You've just changed the sheets. So what exactly are you playing at with me?'

'Listen, Gerry Gretz. There's something about you that just thrills me through and through. It goes right down through me, here, between my breasts, as soon as I hear your voice, even on the telephone. With my boyfriend it's different. He's for weekends, for going shopping on Saturday morning like any normal girl. I like having a man to carry my Provigo bags up here for me. And you'd hate that. So, I have to look elsewhere for that.'

'Yes, but in bed, in bed. Just explain to me what you do with him in bed if I'm the one you like best....'

'He warms me up. He cooks the chicken and you eat it. Now that's enough talk. Come and try out my clean sheets. I keep them in sweet clover, just for you.'

Before he fell asleep, Gretz had time to think to himself, 'She's not all that frigid. I can imagine her writhing under the caresses of another man, but with her head filled with a thousand confused thoughts, guilt, defiance, desire, *let him get it over with as quick as he can, because he's not the one I want*, fantasizing about someone else who may be me, yes, confusion, the meeting-ground of all the contradictions you think you can resolve in the single voice of orgasm, but which leaves you more scrambled than before... and, in the last analysis, that's your truest being, your real self, all that I love you for. The living, suffering incarnation of all the contradictions of this world, incarnation of universal chaos and still in that chaos seeking something that will give it meaning.'

Chapter Five

On the West Island

It happened in one of the nice neighbourhoods where the English live, in the part they started to call the West Island after the victory of that goddamned separatist party, the one that wanted to chop down the beautiful, bounteous, Canada-catalpa tree, and after whose election it was the turn of the English to have to go in search of an identity, because they too were beginning to feel the need of a territory to call their own.

Out on the West Island, a late-model car had blown up while actually roaring down the autoroute, along a stretch that was nicely fenced in on both sides by a very high, efficient chain-link fence, so that the car went plunging into it along quite some distance, like a shark into a net. All that was left of the unlucky driver was a few shreds of flesh that the lab experts and the police would soon be scraping up in bits and pieces, hoping to reconstitute the unfortunate victim from splinters of bone and scraps of hair and pores of skin without the skin – not all of him, but at least enough to identify him.

At first sight, it looked like a bomb under the driver's seat. But for most of the onlookers clustered around the wreckage of the car, English-speakers jerked from the comfortable torpor of a humid July afternoon, there could be no doubt that this was a terrorist who had fallen victim to his own engine of destruction – before he had had a chance to drop it into a West Island mailbox. It was written all over their faces: *So much the better, there's one less, this'll teach the young fanatics a lesson.* One of them even said, in a loud, clear voice, 'Not even bright enough to handle his own bloody bomb properly.'

Gretz's bloody beeper went off: '*Beep-beep*, hurry up, Gretz, it's almost the deadline and this might just be our headline for....' Goddamned beeper stopped short again. But the message was crystal clear. Hurry up. In clearer terms yet, it said, 'Move your ass, Gretz, *hostie*. Give us a break from the sociology before Elliott, the boss, has hysterics.'

So, on his way back to the high-rise hovel, he was already running over his lead in his head: 'Montreal, the Xth of July, nineteen hundred and whatever, somewhere between 69 and 76 (since the paper only lasted five years).'

'What an ironic fate for this young Québécois who, like a modern-day Joan of Arc, dreamed of giving the English a scare and booting them out of Québec, but who has instead left his own torn flesh spread like fertilizer all over their nice green lawns, those same lawns so often reviled as being the ultimate symbol of colonialism when compared with the stinking alleys inhabited by the Pea-Soupers in the East End.'

Like the lawns of India, the lawns of Africa, the greenery of Empire. *Beep-beep*, get the lead out, Gretz, heft your partner and do-si-do and move it as quick as you can.

'Okay, okay, I'm flat out on my flat car and on my way and I won't be late because anyway I never am. I've got two paragraphs of my lead written already.'

But as soon as he set foot in the office, the boss was bellowing at him from the far end of the newsroom.

'Gretz, message for you, very urgent, from Bricaud.'

The message was short but clear.

'Talk to me before you write a word.'

The boss was leaning over his shoulder.

'I've been waiting for the masterpiece. Gimme your two lead paragraphs, I'm gonna shoot them up to composition, twelve-point Bodoni black to fourteen picas.'

'What do you mean, fourteen picas, aren't you running my lead over two columns, with a six-column photo of the mangled Pontiac and a little bit of brain stuck to the windshield?'

'Listen, Gerry, you're not the only one here. There's Baril too. He needs six columns to dump on the Parti Québécois.'

'Why, what have they done now?'

'They're squabbling.'

'Without wishing to deprive Baril and, in all modesty, it seems to me that that's not exactly the scoop of the year compared with my FLQist who's auto-banana-peeled himself.'

'Come on, come on, let's have it *au plus clisse*.'

He meant fucking fast. Elliott had one peculiarity however. He swore like a trooper but he never articulated his swear-words completely. For *Hostie* he said *''stie,'* for *Crisse* he said *'Clisse'*, for *Tabarnacle* he said *'Tabar'*, for *Clitoris* he said *'Clit'*, and for *Ciboire* he said *'Taboire'*. For example, he would say, *'Clisse de Clit', de Tabar de Taboire de Saint-Simone de 'stie.'* Saint Simone was *Saint-Simonaque*, naturally.

'Montreal, the 17th of July, 1974, byline Gretz....'

'What an ironic fate for this young Québécois, whose shredded flesh has just finished its earthly sojourn in the form of fertilizer on a lawn in Ville Mont-Royal which, thanks to him, will now be a little greener than those of the neighbours.'

'But this is christly poetry,' howled Elliott, 'and this is a newspaper we're running here, not a forum for the lucubrations of a *tabar* of a lucubrationist who wants to break up my.... Listen, this isn't yesterday morning at nine-fifteen, this is tonight, Saturday, one hour before deadline, and here I have Gretz showing off his prowess, I mean his poetry!'

'Eet's ze zame zing, boss,' said Gretz.

'Okay, okay, sing but don't try to flatter me.'

'Well, don't splatter me. I had a bath two days ago boss, so watch what you spit out on me. And it was a bath for two, Badedas, with my girlfriend....'

'Who said anything about spit,' said Elliott, 'just shit or get off the pot, that deadline's on the way.'

'Right away.'

'And not just the deadline Gretz, there's also a babe expecting me for supper.'

'Another *crisse* of an over-cooked mushy spaghetti with canned Catelli sauce? Nothing to be in rush about, boss.'

'The facts, Gerry, facts, facts, facts. The five double-yous, who, where, when, why, where....'

'Montreal, 17-07-74, by Gretz.'

'Yesterday a man was killed on the section of autoroute that crosses Ville Mont-Royal when the bomb he was carrying blew up in his car, a late-model Pontiac, pulverizing the front seat on the driver's side, leaving him in shreds of flesh, and sending his car flying out of control into a Frost fence, like an enormous fish in a steel net.'

'No poetry, Gretz. '*Stie*. When I want poetry I'll send you a telegram a week ahead of time. Scrap that paragraph.'

'Watch it boss, time is passing, we'll miss the deadline. Take your pick, either it's poetry and on time or it isn't and we're late.'

'*Clisse*. Master blackmailer. Anyway, put in all the poetry you want, I'll chop it out shortly, on the stone.'

'You're twenty years behind, boss. We don't say stone any more these days, we say Pay Stop, and need I add that in this place it shouldn't be Pay Stop but stop pay because half the time our pay cheques bounce.'

'Listen, if you've got a job somewhere else, don't hesitate, Gretz, because we need you around here about as much as Marilyn needed three tits.'

'Gretz, telephone, *urgentissimo*, it's Bricaud.'

'Yeah, Brique, what's up?'

'You're the one who's on the bomb in the late-model Pontiac in Tee-Aime-Arr?'

(TMR, Town of Mount Royal, in French Ville Mont-Royal.)

'Yes I am, why?'

'And you've also started cooking up an FLQ story by now I suppose?'

'Who told you that, Bricaud?'

'That's what all you cretins are writing in all the Montreal papers these days.'

'Thanks a lot, Monsieur Bricaud.'

'It's from the heart. So drop that right away, it's not worth shit. Leave all that stuff to the

English papers, they're all biased fools. But to you, I'm giving the true truth.'

'Okay, okay, don't keep me dangling, what is the true truth?'

'Don't think I'm going to tell you over the blower, knothead, this is something to whisper in your ear.'

'Where are you? I'm on my way.'

'In the Gobelet, back room, under the big scythe.'

'And where are you off to Gretz, my *tab de saint-sim*?'

'His cuss-words are getting shorter all the time,' thought Gretz. 'Day'll come when he won't talk at all.'

'Listen Elliott, Brique is gonna give me the whole story. It's either that or making up some christly thing as usual. What do you prefer, that or bullshit?'

'Okay, go on *'stie*, but make it quick, you know what they say in Paris, *fais-ça fissa*, on the double.'

'Look, boss, why don't you call your girl-friend and tell her to turn down all the burners except for the one she's got lit up for you? Order in your usual from Laurier Barbecue, chef salad on the side, and tell her that you're bringing supper. She'll like that. She'll think you're starting to be less macho.'

'Ah fuck you, Gerry Gretz.'

Le Gobelet was one of the sacred places of initiation into folkloric Québec. The walls were covered with the tools of our ancient French ancestors. Hardwood hay forks, manure forks, shit shovels, sap dippers and hay saws.

As Gretz got there, the waiter said to him, 'Gerry, call your boss at the office. It's marked *fissa*, as they say in Constantine.'

'Hello, boss. Gretz here, what's the emergency?'

'I checked and you're right, nobody says stone any more, and nobody talks about carding, or lead, or linotypes, or Heidelberg presses. But *hic et nunc* they don't say Pay Stop any more either, but Paste Up, because Paste is *colle*, you know, glue. So you can just take back all those humiliating puns about robber or rubber cheques from the co-op, because we've been putting up with you here for nearly five years.'

'Or else...?'

'Or else I give priority to Baril's story about the Montreal Centre dust-up over whether or not they need a hyphen between sovereignty and association.'

'Okay, okay, I take it all back.'

To kill time, Gretz was writing his name, address and postal code in his new appointment book when finally Inspector Bricaud pulled out the chair beside him.

'Okay, listen to me, Gretz. This has nothing to do with any FLQ bomb or any terrorist blowing himself up by accident, it's a girl.'

'A girl? *Tabarna*, that means my lead is wrong from start to finish!'

'I told you not to write a word before I could talk to you, didn't I?'

'Yiss-yiss-yiss, you told me, Inspector Bricaud, pliss forgive me. So the true truth is that...?'

'It was some little girl from the Maf' who'd gone out to deliver a few lines of coke for the weekend to all her faithful English customers on the West Island.'

'But what about the bomb?'

'Good question, the latest thing with that crowd, came straight from New York, special delivery in the diplomatic bag.'

'And the little girl, as you call her, who would want to blow her up?'

'My hypothesis is that she was a courier until just recently, but that she'd decided to set up in business for herself with the customers she got from her wholesaler. And shoplifting is theft, in case you don't remember. Lifting the boss's coke and then taking his customers too, was definitely a no-no, as you can probably see.'

'Yes, I can see that,' said Gretz. 'But tell me, Inspector, why are you giving this to me?'

'In memory of the illegal distilleries, my young friend. And besides, I'm beginning to think they're blaming just a little bit too much on those kids in the FLQ.'

He brought it all back, the country stills. Gretz remembered it well. It was in Palimpseste, the little provincial city where he had begun his brilliant career by reporting on run-over dogs and the drunks at the municipal courthouse.

One day, at Bricaud's request, he had needled a judge who was handing down sentences that really were too light, to the guys who were selling their own specially distilled holy water, homemade in an abandoned cow-shed somewhere.

'Is Your Seigneurial Highness, Judge Langlois, aware of the fact that, among the customers of the man you convicted two days ago, four have gone blind, seven are impotent, and nine others are well on their way to Alzheimer's?'

In those days, Bricaud was a Mountie, and he was in it because illegal alcohol was a question of excise taxes. But now he was a provincial motorcycle cop.

'Tabaslak!' said Gretz, casting a glance at the Gobelet's handsome Black Horse clock with its halo of green neon, the colour of beer after the sixth Dow, you remember, the beer that kills. 'Have to report back to Elliott, he must really be having hysterics by now.'

'Oh come on, Gretz, calm down,' said Bricaud. 'With a scoop like that, you're easy, you've got lots of time to have another.'

'Hi boss, Gretz here. I've got the whole story on the bomb in the Town of Mount Royal, a scoop from a former Mountie, and I've already....'

'Yeah, yeah, I know, you've written the lead,' said Elliott. 'In poetry or in journalism?'

'In journalism, of course,' said Gretz. 'This is twenty years of experience you're talking to, Monsieur, so show a little respect. Anyway, boss, I'll be there in a flash, just the time it takes to jump into my Pontiac and I'll be with you. Pull out the choke on my old Royal so I won't have to waste time warming it up.'

'You are going to find me in such a *Crisse de Chrisologue* of a rage that there's steam coming out of my nose-holes and my ear-flaps and you won't have to worry about warming anything up. Everything here is red-hot: the typewriters, the chairs, the telephones, the pencils and the rolls of teletype paper. The only thing cold is my all-dressed pizza from George's, which my girlfriend is waiting for with less and less patience. When I get there, what she pulls out from under her skirt won't be her panties but a sawed-off twelve-gauge to blow me against the wall with the rest of her antiques.'

'And you'll become part of our national heritage, and one day we'll find you hung up at the Gobelet.'

'Ah-ha. So that's where you are, my *tabar de clisse de saint-Clit' de monaque d'hostie toastée*. Listen, the deadline was six minutes ago. If you're not down here in ten minutes max, you can expect to finish with a bomb up your rear too.'

'Montreal, 17-07-74, by Gretz....'
'A settling of accounts in the drug community took the life of a young girl this afternoon at about four o'clock, when a remote-controlled bomb went off under the driver's seat of her car just after she had finished her cocaine deliveries to a gilded West Island clientele. Following the explosion, the car continued at a high speed, tearing out a considerable length of the chain-link fence that separates the express lanes of the ring road from the comfortable neighbourhoods alongside. Without the link fence, which wrapped itself around the victim's car like a spider web, the machine would have kept straight on into the Jones's swimming pool, the Joneses themselves being among the coke lady's customers.'

'Thus the rising tide of decadence has begun to take effect even within the social class which dominated Québec for so many years.'

'I warn you, Gretz. I'm cutting out that last part. We're not doing sociology here, this is journalism.'

'You really do want to stifle all your employees' fun, don't you?'

'You've stifled enough of mine tonight. While you were knocking back a last gobelet at the Gobelet, my girlfriend called me to say it was all over between us, she's had enough of waiting at home for me on Saturday nights and she's changed the lock on her door.'

'Well, there's a girl who must have loved you *en saint-simonaque*. One day you'll thank me for giving you the chance to see her in her true colours. When she was lucky enough to have an Elliott in her bed and in her life, she should have been willing to put up with the priority he would naturally give to the noble profession of journalism over some silly social convention about getting there on time to eat cold pizza.'

Chapter Six

The Lesbos

Years before, Gretz had been in the habit of going to the Lesbos, which was a restaurant where you never saw anyone but men. It was Inspector Kolokotronis's favourite haunt. The walls were plastered with scenic photographs of Greece's most beautiful sights and the Acropolis cropped up everywhere.

'You should visit Greece, Monsieur Gretz,' said the owner, a certain Clitoridis. 'I'm telling you, that's the place. Greece is the country of flowers, so many of them that bees come from all over Europe to gather their nectar there. On their way home, in fact, lots of the little creatures just drop into the sea because their feet are so heavy with pollen. Their cadavers wash up on the beaches in the thousands.'

'Thousands?'

'Oh yes, Monsieur Gretz, and if you ever go there, don't drive with your car windows rolled down.'

'Why not?'

'Because the air is so loaded with perfume that after a few kilometers, you'll be completely drunk. Even just an ordinary police check will catch you with an excess of alcohol in your blood, and then you'll lose your licence and have to make the rest of your trip on foot.'

'I'll have the *calamari*,' said Gretz, 'with lots of garlic.'

'*Anch'io,*' said Kolokotronis. 'So you're in love, Gerry.'

'Not really, Kolo. As you know, Monsieur l'Inspecteur, love is a big word.'

'You've been seen going into her place, more than once.'

'What? You've been having me followed?'

'Not you, you pretentious twit. Her. We've spread a net right around the Wolfrid Milton gang and as you may know, she's been delivering for him. But I warn you, that's a state secret, or else no more contacts for you.'

'Oh come on, Kolo, when have I ever double-crossed you?'

'Never, that's a fact. But you know, love changes everything.'

'I'm telling you, I'm not in love.'

'Well anyway, if ever it turns into love, let me know so I can prepare for the worst. Tell me, what's so wonderful about her?'

'Ah, the mouth she's got.... I'm telling you, Kolo, you can eat and drink in it. Her lips are like apricots. Her tongue is a heat-seeking missile.'

'Without the nuclear tip I hope.'

'No, the nuclear tip is me, when she takes hold of it.'

'What about her skin, Gretz, tell me about her skin.'

'Have you ever tried reading Braille?'

'Nope.'

'When I touch her, my ol' Kolo, her skin comes up all over in goose bumps, just like Braille. So, I try to read what her skin is saying to me and it's always the same message: make love to me, Monsieur Gretz.'

'So her skin even calls you Monsieur?'

'Yes, Monsieur.'

'Has she told you that you're the first one who's ever made her come?'

'Who told you that? Have you got microphones in her walls? But you couldn't have, that's mediaeval....'

'Mediaeval, why?'

'Because you're as thick as a stone wall from the Middle Ages.'

'My dear Gerry, what makes you think I would have needed a microphone in her bedroom wall to know she told you that?'

'Believe me, Kolo, she's a mutant.'

'You mean a woman who's renounced all female failings? That's something I'd like to see, tell me about it.'

'The other evening I got to her place two hours late. Know what she said to me?'

'No, remember, I don't have any microphones in her walls....'

'She threw her arms around my neck and smothered my excuses with a French kiss and said that it was a lucky thing, actually, because she had work to finish. How many women do you know who'd react like that? Or just to keep it within the bounds of reality, let's take your wife as an example, the lovely Hermione, has she ever said anything like that to you when you were late?'

'Please, Gretz, please, let's keep Hermione out of this discussion. I want to be able to digest my *calamari*.'

'Even Lesbos *calamari*?'

'Yes, even Lesbos *calamari*.'

'Know what she said to me in bed one day?'

'Nope.'

'She said, you are to my cunt what Blühmel is to the trumpet.'

'What Blühmel would that be?' asked Kolo, pulling a squid bone out of his mouth, delicate as the wing of a dragon-fly, and laying it on the edge of his plate.

'He's the one who invented fingerplay. Listen, Kolo, what really got me, about her, are her eyes. The first time I saw her I couldn't tell, not even when I stared at her, if they were grey or blue. It all depends on the sky, on the level of luminosity. So with her you don't have to listen to the weather reports. When it's cloudy, her eyes are blue. When it's sunny, they're grey. And to keep you guessing, she makes them up. When they're grey, she uses a blue liner and when they're blue, she uses grey. End result, every time you look into her eyes, you go head over heels.'

'But grey is a cold colour, my old friend.'

'When her eyes are cold, her body is burning hot, and when her eyes are warm, it's her body that's cool.'

'I don't see what's so great about that,' said Kolo.

'What's great, ol'Kolo, is that you never know where you are with her, and that's what I like. She can change her mind from one second to the next.'

'So, she's just a capricious little bitch.'

'No, Kolo, she wants to know if you really love her or if it's just for the sex. And in her case it's for real.'

'What's for real?'

'It's for real that she really wants to know.'

'Okay, okay,' said Kolo. 'While I'm thinking of it, do you know what language the expression *okay* comes from?'

'It's American obviously.'

'No, no, not at all. It comes from Greek, from *oli kala*, which means *all correct*.'

'Can you prove that?'

'No more than you can prove to me that you're not in love.'

When he got back to the police station, Kolo warned his men.

'Watch out for Gretz, he's in love, he may blow up in our faces at any moment.'

As Gerry got back to Gri-Gri's place he told her, 'I made Kolo think that I'm in love with you, so be careful.'

Chapter Seven

The Hotels

To foil any possible watchers, Gerry and Gri-Gri would meet in anonymous hotel rooms in and around Palimpseste. Décors *à la chinoise* with huge fans pinned to the wall over the bed, Mexican interiors, fake Moorish arches. Everywhere, on cardboard textured to imitate the artists' brush strokes, there were reproductions of Rembrandt or Van Gogh. But the uglier the rooms were, the more passionately they loved each other in them, and the more hostile the world around them was, the greater was the value of their coming together. It was at such times that their feelings of being alone in the world were at their strongest, and their convictions at their clearest that, at that moment, without each other they would die.

In those soulless, depersonalized rooms, the epitome of bad taste and devoid of all that was human, they were more desperate still, plunged deeper yet into their distress – and hurling themselves at each other all the more furiously, as if their bodies, their very skins, were more than ever their protection against the world beyond themselves. As if each one's arms closed around the other could block out their ultimate extinction, their imminent non-being, the non-love before and after them, and the ugliness which surrounded them like a distillation of all the ugliness in the world. As if they would never see each other again. As if, as if....

They had to go beyond the limits of anguish and confusion to discover the extent to which their love was their only fixed point and their only refuge.

Chapter Eight

The Hold-Up

As Inspector Kolokotronis stepped into the press room at the police station, there was a veritable explosion of cameras. *Click, bzzz, click, bzzz* and *click bzzz*. Kolokotronis, Kolo for old-time reporters like Gerry Gretz, loved every moment of this ritual. 'Just like a prime minister,' he told himself as he stepped up to the microphone.

'Gentlemen, we have a body and a half on our hands as the result of a very strange hold-up, something unprecedented even in this city where we thought we'd seen every crime in the book, from the case of the headless man in the Rue Bourbonnière to the arrest of Wilbert Coffin in a downtown rooming house.'

'And ladies...!' said someone in the room.

'I beg your pardon?' said the inspector.

'You have to say *ladies and gentlemen* now,' said Josée-Anne Grognon. 'The days of your headless man in the rue Bourbonnière are long gone.'

'If there were any ladies here, I would have noticed...,' the inspector came back at her.

But she cut him off.

'Monsieur l'Inspecteur,' she said, 'considering the remarkable performance of your department over the last few months, the cops might do well to handle their few solid contacts with the local press a little more delicately.'

'Okay, okay,' said the inspector. 'A big bad macho I may be, and born in Manni where we never back down, but I apologize, I was wrong.'

Then he laid out on the table a file folder containing nothing but two computer print-out sheets and he went on.

'According to our reconstruction of events, which is as faithful as we can make it, we are able to tell you that this is what happened: the incident took place in the parking lot of the Van Horne Shopping Centre and the victim, Sylvio Debs, who was known to police, was at the wheel of a brick-red 1967 Plymouth Duster with the engine running. Despite the fact that it was a very cold day, the window on the driver's side was rolled right down. A hundred and fifty feet away was a small branch of the Canadian National Bank. It was two o'clock in the afternoon, or fourteen hundred hours if you want it in Celsius. It was the time of day when the guys at the bank....'

'And the women, Inspector Kolo...!'

It was Josée-Anne interrupting again.

'As far as I know, Mademoiselle Grognon, my name is still Kolokotronis, as these journalistic gentlemen will attest.'

'Yup,' said Gerry Gretz, 'for the last forty-nine years.'

'That part is my business, Gretz.'

'*Oli kala*, Kolo,' said Gretz, who had picked up twenty or so words of modern Greek somewhere.

'So it was the time of day when the people who work behind the counter in the bank come back from lunch dreaming about taking a nice little siesta. At one of the wickets another individual who is also known to police, a certain Mario Marcotte, arrived with a semi-automatic in his fist to withdraw the contents of the cashdrawer or, to be more precise, exactly fourteen thousand, eight hundred dollars. It was pay day for employees of the government and there was a lot more cash in the till than there would have been on any other day. Marcotte and Debs, who used to be civil servants themselves, were well aware of that fact. Then Marcotte bundled the money into a double-strength Glad bag and raced out of the bank at top speed in the direction of the Duster. He threw the Glad bag in through the open window and it landed on the seat on the passenger side, the seat sometimes referred to as the suicide seat.'

'But now you'd better tie your tuques down with baling wire because this is where things start to get complicated. Debs steps on the gas, expecting Marcotte to jump into the car while it's starting to roll. Then, catastrophe or the luck of the draw, one of the bank's customers pulls out of a parking space and cuts off the Duster.

Debs slams on the brakes and the back end of the Duster wallops Mario Marcotte, slams him onto the icy street and he slides half under the car.'

'Sylvio Debs figures that time is precious so he takes off again and this time he drives right over Mario Marcotte's legs. Everybody in the shopping centre heard his scream of pain and it's still giving them the shivers. But Marcotte, on the ground and with the left side of his head covered with blood, aims his semi-automatic after the Duster and fires through the car door. We found three of the four slugs. It was the fourth one that killed Sylvio Debs. It was the kind with a soft tip. The entry wound in the victim's body was no bigger than my little finger....'

The inspector held a hairy finger up.

'...but when the bullet reached muscle and cartilage, the point flattened. It blew poor Debs's heart to mush and the exit wound was a ragged, messy hole a good five inches across.'

'The Duster kept going for another five hundred feet and stopped all by itself when it came up against the parking attendant's kiosk; he was the eye witness who gave my guys the details so we could reconstruct the incident the way I've just described it to you. Inside the Duster, we found Debs with his head on the Glad bag, just like it was a feather pillow. Any questions, lady and gentlemen?'

'Inspector Kolo,' Gerry Gretz wanted to know, 'what kind of shape is the other suspect in at the present time?'

'Right now he's in intensive care at the Hôtel Dieu in Montreal. They've done a CAT scan on him and I'm waiting for the results. We want to question him as soon as possible. But it's only the doctors who can give us that authorization.'

'What's your theory about the reasons Marcotte might have had for wanting to do a job on Sylvio Debs?'

'I haven't got one theory, I've got several. Did he think Debs hit him on purpose? Or did something happen between them in the weeks before the hold-up that might explain a settling of accounts? The only one who can tell us is Marcotte.'

Chapter Nine

The Black Bird

Wolfrid Milton was at his wit's end because a starling had got into the house, which was a very bad omen. Therefore he had an unending stream of choice things to say to his mother, to the maid and to his children. He put the whole family through the wringer for having left the sliding glass doors to the yard wide open.

'Even when I told you, you gang of nit-wits. With a nest in the crotch of the locust tree, it was clear as day that that bird was bound to want to come in and see what was going on in the house.'

'But above all,' Wolfrid yelled, 'he mustn't be killed inside. That'd be a sign of really big trouble. We've got to catch him alive.'

In their attempts to corner the bird, they were all waving sheets or curtains or bedspreads, making a racket like the sails of a three-masted schooner flapping loose in a high wind. Yet all this activity, far from trapping the bird, served only to frighten him still more.

'Here birdy, birdy, birdy,' carolled fat Wolfrid in a choir-boy's treble. But, as soon as Wolfrid's thick sausage fingers came anywhere near the birdy, the poor creature would panic all over again and fly blindly towards the light, brutally smashing its head against the windowpanes. In its fright it was now dropping splotches of terrified bird shit as well.

From one failed grab to the next, Wolfrid was beginning to lose patience. He had started with sweetness and cosiness, even baptizing the bird with the cute nickname of Boswell, in memory of a beer long vanished from the market but whose name could still bring forth tears of nostalgia. Boswell was given a diminutive.

'Here Boswi, Boswi, little bitty-bird, come here, we aren't going to hurt you, we just want to let you out. Be nice with your little ol' nuncle Wollie.'

But the bird preferred his nuncle Wollie as far off as possible. Hence the change of tone.

'You little *tabarnaque* of a birdbrain, shitting all over the furniture, if I get my hands on you, I'll pluck the feathers off of you all right, my *hostie*.'

'*Alouette,*' said Steve, Wolfrid's son.

Wolfrid did not waste any time mulling over that remark. Now it was his hand that flew – and clouted Steve in the chops.

'Old man's a bit grouchy this morning,' said Steve.

'Listen kid, a black bird in the house is no joke. It means seven years of bad luck. But naturally you young ones don't give a damn about any of that, because you have no respect for anything any more anyway.'

Boswell, all ruffled and torn, was by this time perched on the fake crystal chandelier in the Milton's dining room, and Wolfrid, with his mouth full of curses, had climbed onto a leather hassock. Boswell turned his head towards Wolfrid and sighted down his long yellow beak. As Wolfrid's hand came dangerously close, Boswell jabbed his beak into the Tomatis point, the soft spot between the thumb and the index finger of his right hand. At which Wolfrid lost his balance, fell over backwards and on his way down cracked his head on one of the fins of his big wing chair. Blood came spurting out of a long gash down his forehead and he let out a howl that would have taken the leaves off the trees. Boswell was terrified and abandoned his perch to fly straight into the bullet-proof pane between the dining room and the yard. His head made a nasty little *bonk*, and he fell back soundlessly onto the Oriental carpet. In an avalanche of blasphemy, Wolfrid bent and gathered up the small pile of motionless feathers. Then he wound up with a good swing and hurled it outside. For just a moment the wings of the dead bird opened and for one last time, as he had in the best years of his youth, Boswell rode the air again, the uncertain air of a cold March evening, with absolutely no destination in mind.

At the same instant the telephone rang. It was a telephone with a marble base and a gold-plated hook for the receiver.

'Wouldn't you know it,' said Wolfrid. 'Hello, this is Wolfrid Milton, starling killer, and what can I do for you?'

'Hey, this is no time for jokes, boss. Bad news. Sylvio Debs got shot this PM. Three slugs in him, one of them right smack in the West-clock. What do I do?'

'Above all, nothing, you *saint-ciboulette de patate frette*. Close all the windows at the office. If you see a starling anywhere near, blast it with a twelve-gauge. Don't take any christly chances with the little buggers. They don't look like much but they can ruin your life from top to bottom. But anyway, but anyway. The harm's done. No good crying about it now. At Sandhurst they always said to pray to God and keep your powder dry. So don't let's take any chances. Double the guard on the roof of the store and on the house across the street.'

In keeping with his custom, Wolfrid did not get into bed that night until he had looked through the day's newspapers. In the horoscope column, under Pisces, he read: *Business: one of your associates puts you into a difficult position*. That was Sylvio Debs. *Health: avoid sugary desserts. On the social scene: escape boredom by accepting invitations from friends*. As long as that doesn't mean jail, he thought. Then at the end he found the only good note for the day, which was that *fish* (fish, as everyone knows, in Latin is Pisces) *never cry*.

Chapter Ten

Physiotherapy

The lady doctor set her stopwatch.

'Okay, Monsieur Marcotte, let's see you screw these nuts onto these bolts.'

This was the great Mario Marcotte, M.M., as he was called and who always said, yes, M.M. just like in Marilyn Monroe. The great M.M. himself, whose curriculum *vitré* was as long as your arm, detailing not only the *collèges classiques* and the boarding schools where he had received his education, but also the sentences he had received and the prisons where he had served them. Yet here was the great Marcotte himself, two hundred pounds at his very skinniest, sitting like a good little boy in front of a small board which bristled with a forest of little bolts in different sizes. Right beside it was a tumulus of nuts. His assignment today was to screw these nuts onto these bolts, he who had spent his life carrying out far more absorbing assignments, such as leaving the scene of a robbery at breakneck speed, skillfully using his knowledge of the back alleys and one-way streets of the Plateau Mont-Royal to elude the cops, a slower-moving species whose only assignment was to defend the belongings of others.

He thought to himself that he had really done everything but kill.

Damned liar, whispered the remnants of his conscience.

'Now you have to do it all over again with your left hand, since the injury which you suffered damaged the right side of your brain.'

The great Marcotte started over again and, finding the fingers of his left hand very numb, dropped the nut, changed hands, said *tabarnacle* and got his knuckles rapped.

'You remind me of the Reverend Mother Marcelle,' he told the doctor lady.

'Who's that?' asked the Monblanc woman.

'She was a *Fille de Jésus*, from the bunch we used to call pissy-French-from-France. She was the one who tortured me when I was a pupil in kindergarten.'

Here he was, thinking he was finished for life, as good as dead, since he had had what he called his 'tumour', and now be damned if he hadn't caught himself looking at the nurse Monblanc with an ever-mounting sexual interest. When she crossed her legs under her desk, he strained his ears to hear the sound of her nylons rubbing together, up at the top around her thighs. He pushed a pencil off the edge of the desk, hoping to catch a glimpse of more of her when he bent to pick it up.

'So nurse, what are you planning to do with me today?'

'I'm not a nurse, I'm a psychologist,' the Damsel responded, in a tone which did not invite repartee. 'I want to check your dexterity in fine manipulations.'

Fine manipulations..., thought Marcotte, I could show you some fine manipulations all right, just about where your panty hose has a line between thick and thin.

'Here's the instrument,' she said, setting another little board down in front of him, this one with the upper part of a shoe attached to it, the part that covers the instep. On each side was a flap with a row of ten eyelets covering a shoe-tongue. The shoe-tongue looked strange all by itself like that, without a shoe.

'So what now?' said Mario.

'You thread the shoelace into the eyelets, doing the eyelets on the right with your right hand and the eyelets on the left with your left hand, without mixing them up or we'll start over again, and when you've finished, you tie a nice neat bow.'

'With both hands?'

'Of course.'

She had her stop-watch in her hand.

'Ready?'

'Ready,' said Mario.

The *tick-tack, tick-tack, tick-tack* brought back memories of the mechanism in the bomb he had used to blow the door off the safe in the bank in Mascouche. That was at his bank-robber's graduation, twenty years before.

The left hand worked pretty well, it was the right one that kept giving him a hard time.

'Now do it for me with the other hand.'

When he tried with his right hand, it was as if the shoelace were physically refusing to go into the eyelets. It balked like a myopic tailor's thread that did not want to be threaded through the needle.

'Stay calm, Monsieur Marcotte,' the Monblanc thing said to him. 'We have our whole lives in front of us.'

'Yeah, especially me,' said Mario, 'with the sentence I've got.'

'With your right hand now,' she said.

The *tick-tack* of the stop-watch did not seem to be counting the seconds, it was dropping them off, like beads off a broken necklace.

'That's a lot slower, Monsieur Marcotte, forty seconds longer.'

But the bow was a beauty. The centre was a real little viper all perfectly twisted around itself and the two loops on either side spread out like the wings of a dragonfly.

'Goddamned shoelace,' he said, angrily.

'Don't get mad,' she said in her psychological tone. 'It's perfectly normal. This isn't a test of speed, it's a way for me to check from week to week to see if you're making progress. You'll see, in X months, there won't be any difference.'

'Will I be better?'

'Better than whom?' she asked.

'Better than now,' said Marcotte.

'You'll be down to less than two minutes to tie your shoes, anyway. Besides,' she said, 'it's really just as well for you to start from so far back, because your progress will be a lot more encouraging for you.'

'So I should have taken ten minutes to do it.'

Mario tried to see through her white nurse's blouse, to find out if she was wearing a bra.

'Could you lend me your stop-watch?'

'What for?'

'To see how long it takes me to find out if you're wearing a bra on your pretty little pink breasts.'

'Monsieur Marcotte,' she said, putting her hands over her breasts.

'Listen, Miss Monblanc, I've been locked up for six months and they only let me out of prison to come and see you. Try to understand.'

'Let's go on to the second test. This is a memory test. I read you a news item from the paper and you tell me what was in it with as many details as possible.'

'In Des Carrières Lane, a delivery truck is parked. A thief steals part of the stock from the back of the truck. He puts the stolen goods into the trunk of a car which is parked nearby with the engine running. He jumps into the car, but not without first locking the back of the truck with a brand new padlock.'

'Where'd you find that story?'

'In a manual of tests.'

Mario was astounded. The story was his own story and he was the thief.

'Okay, I'm going to tell you that story the way it really happened. The truck was carrying sides of beef, Western beef. It had *Western Meat Packers* written on the side of the truck. I'd been following the truck for an hour and I knew that it was going to stop for exactly eight minutes in Des Carrières Lane because that's what it did every morning. I too used to work with a stop-watch. Each side of beef was worth two hundred dollars. The padlock was a special model with rubber panties on it to prevent rust. As soon as the truck was parked, I raced over with my bolt-cutters, snipped off the padlock in a jiffy, opened the doors, took out two sides of beef which I put into the trunk of my old Pontiac and then locked my own padlock, which was exactly like the one I'd cut off, onto the doors of the truck. But you missed one detail. There was a young woman coming out of her place through the lane who saw the whole thing. She was standing there in shock and then, just as I expected, she started to lecture me. But I knew exactly what to say to her. I told her, listen lady, it's the insurance company that pays Western Meat anyway. Besides, I'm not like them, I've never stolen anything from the poor. So, she let me get away. Now tell me, what do you think of my memory?'

'I'll have to discuss this with Dr. Bakunin. You're really not an ordinary patient, Monsieur Marcotte. In a case like yours, I'm not sure if all our tests are valid.'

Chapter Eleven

Menier Chocolate

The Prime Minister, upon whom Her Majesty the Queen had conferred the title of Lord-Qui-Pète-Et-Qui-Rote-Dans-Le-Trou-d'Eau, lifted the receiver of the telephone which was down there in front of him, attached at knee level to the circular table in the ministerial council chamber, and spoke to the woman at the candy kiosk on the left as you enter the Parliament Buildings.

'*Bonjour,* Madame, this is the Prime Minister speaking. I trust you are in a position to provide me with my habitual meal?'

A few moments later a page in a burgundy jacket brought him his chocolate bar. This was all he would eat during the day. Turning to his colleagues, Lord-Qui-Rote said to them: 'This is a chocolate which is absolutely pure, unadulterated by almonds, raisins, or any sweetening agent whatsoever.'

Meanwhile, the page stood there waiting, shifting from foot to foot. Finally, he muttered out a few words to the Prime Minister in such a hurried voice that what he said couldn't be made out.

'Ah yes, yes, to be sure,' said Lord-Qui-Rote. 'I suppose you'd like me to settle up with you. But how much are these selling for now?'

'Eighty-seven cents,' said the page.

'I beg your pardon?' said the Prime Minister.

To which the page, after taking a deep breath and inflating himself with air all the way down to his diaphragm, as taught to him in pages' training school, said again, detaching each syllable as if it were a separate word: 'Eight-ee sev-en cents, Mr. Pry Minister....'

'My goodness, have they raised the price again?'

'Monsieur Catholique's new tax...,' said the page.

At this the Prime Minister was overcome with mirth and wagged a vengeful index finger in the direction of Jean Catholique, his Finance Minister. Then, digging into the deepest recesses of his pocket, he fished out and lined up on the table in front of the page the eighty-seven cents, quite a lot of it in coppers.

Nervously, the page hung around to see if the Prime Minister would hand over a few more pennies as a tip, but he waited in vain.

The chocolate bar itself was large and imposing, wrapped in beautiful acid-green paper and covered with gold medals, decorations won at a variety of international exhibitions, Paris in 1900 and Philadelphia in 1876. The Prime Minister laid it in the exact centre of his desk blotter. Then he turned it over, gold medals under, and commenced the unwrapping. He unstuck the paper with a respectful delicacy reminiscent of a celebrant of the Mass unfolding the sacramental towel. Then came the silver foil. When at last the chocolate itself emerged, he paused and leaned back into the depths of his armchair, savouring it in contemplation. Finally, he broke off two squares which he set out with care to the right of the pad of paper that he used for taking notes and on which he wrote down the names of those wishing to speak, one by one as they raised their hands.

He folded the silver paper back over the rest of the chocolate and slid the package into the pocket of his brown jacket with the fine white stripes. He picked up the telephone again.

'Tell me, Madame, how much are the bars of Menier pure baking chocolate selling for? Eighty-seven cents, really! Thank you very much, Madame.'

Turning to his colleagues he said, 'I can assure you, dear colleagues, of what the most exhaustive experiments of Kousmine and Sheldon have proved, that there is nothing but good to be accomplished by eating very little in the middle of the day. It is an excellent way to keep your mind clear and your head cool. Many is the time that I have tried this out on my own metabolism, and I have myself observed that if you damned well lay off, yes, that's what I said, if you damned well lay off your digestive system and your intestinal system for just a few hours, then the energies of your body and of your brain, not being diverted to those lower functions, will naturally be better able to concentrate exclusively on the brain's neuronal and synaptic activity, consequently rendering it quicker and more agile.'

'You will have noticed as well that this is no ordinary chocolate, that this is by no means a chocolate for the riff-raff or the *hoi polloi*, but that it is in fact Menier baking chocolate, the best, the one and only, if I may say so. It is made in France, in the Noisiel factory, and has been since 1825, which is to say forty-two years before the founding of our great country, peopled with our beloved Rocky Mountain bighorns and with the globe's most gigantic mammal, the fin-back whale from the cold waters of the gulf of this very province which is now talking about cutting the umbilical cord. If there are those among you, from either side of the Borden line, who are ready to renounce the fin-back whale or our beloved bighorn sheep, well all I can say is that that is not and will never be my case.'

Then, waxing lyrical, he declaimed:

I wandered, hands plunged in torn pockets,
And O Muse I was your vassal!
My overcoat too was becoming ideal
And la! what splendid loves did I dream
All unaware that bighorn sheep and fin-back whales
Would be my Dulcineas.*

---

* In the original French, this poem bears some resemblance to Rimbaud's 'Ma Bohème' but not much (Translator's note).

'The bitterness of this chocolate is a source of intense satisfaction to me,' he continued, 'for this chocolate, if it contained sugar, would naturally garner the coarse enthusiasm of the common people, whereas by reason of its bitterness, it stands above the importunate and beyond the grasp of those who are unable to show themselves worthy of its qualities.'

'Bitterness,' he insisted, 'is to quality chocolate what quills are to the porcupine or culture to the statesman. Whoever gets too close, gets pricked.'

'Apart from total immersion courses on Menier chocolate, what else went on in those meetings, Mizz Rempart des Béguines?'

(Because in those days nobody said Mamzelle, or Miss, or Madame, but Mizz.)

'As in buzz, Gerry?'

'Zactly, old pal. She was deathly serious about things like that. As they say in Palimpseste, it was a case of Sinny-Quoi-Nun.')

'Young man are you listening to me?'

'I'm doing nothing but that, Mizz,' said Gerry Gretz.

'So the Boss would walk in, always on time. As far as he was concerned, punctuality was absolutely sacred. For a while he even thought of bolting the doors of the Council of Ministers at exactly one minute past the time set for the meeting. And too bad for those who didn't make it. But he tried that once and when all heads were counted, he found himself face to face with two junior ministers. Therefore the experiment lasted no longer than the life of a rose, which is to say one evening. But he'd begin every meeting with the same words: "Punctuality, ladies and gentlemen, is the manners of the...."

'...of the gods, I know, I know. For mercy's sake, there's no need to inflict it on me yet another time, *una volta di più*. But tell me, what's a junior minister, exactly?'

'A pee-wee.'

'I see.'

'Just let me tell you how he carried on while we were working on the referendum campaign. He said to us, with this air of inspiration, that the whole operation had to be seen as a war and that in that connection there were in the history of humanity several shining examples which he was going to quote for us *tout de suite*.'

And The Mizz had said to herself, 'He's off again.'

'First example,' he said, 'the Doges of Venice.'

'The Dodges...?'

Jean Catholique, dumb as ever, did not understand.

'At the time of the Crusader attack against the Most Serene Republic, namely Venice, do you have any idea, is there anyone in this room where people walk in and out at any time of the day or night as if it were Grand Central Station, is there anyone here capable of telling us of the manner in which the Doge and his councillors, your counterparts, gentlemen, ladies, and you too Mizz, have you any idea of the way in which they went about vanquishing the Crusaders?'

'So naturally,' said the Mizz, 'no one had the slightest idea. Besides, even if they had, no one would have dared to say a word for fear of depriving the Boss of his pleasure. But anyway, no one had a clue, whereas he'd probably spent the night swatting it up with his research assistants.'

'Well, it seems that what the Doge did was to start a rumour that the plague was sweeping the region. There was nothing to it of course, or what kind of victory would that have been? But the Crusaders were terrified. They lifted the siege and they all went home.'

Mizz Rempart des Béguines added, 'I just knew that after the Doge of Venice would come Napoleon. And I was right.'

Chapter Twelve

Kutuzov

'Next question, lady and gentlemen – what was the the sublimest, the most extraordinary, the most cogent fruit of the genius of Napoleon Buonaparte as a military leader?'

('Was his Italian accent important?' Gerry wanted to know.

'Absolutely of course, as well as the sort of irritated nasal tone that tinged his voice, like an added attribute of nobility and superiority, just to show the cretins, the *stronzi* and *stronze* that we all were in his eyes, that he knew it all whereas we, we knew nothing, what am I saying, less than nothing.')

'It was at the battle of Austerlitz, called, in the history of the great battles of humanity, the battle of the Emperors because there were three of them present – the Emperor Napoleon, the Czar Alexander of Russia and the Emperor of Austria. The Russian army at the time was under the orders of General Kutuzov and, as it happened, General Kutuzov had discovered that there was a weak point in the battle order of Napoleon's army, drawn up as they were along a chain of three frozen lakes. Kutuzov was certain that all he needed to do to break Napoleon's front and put his army to flight was to send a detachment of his cavalry into this breach at the right moment.'

'Where's the genius in that?' asked Jean Catho.

He'd sensed that the boss was waiting for just such a question in order to be better able to lay out before us, mental retardates that we all were, his infinite knowledge.

'The genius, my friends,' Lord-Qui-Pète-Et-Qui-Rote-Dans-le-Trou-d'Eau went on with delight, 'the genius, as I was saying, consisted in Napoleon Buonaparte's letting Kutuzov believe, in giving him reason to believe, that that particular flank of his army was exposed, so that Kutuzov would direct his attack towards it. There remained nothing more than to wait patiently that Kutuzov might fall into the trap.'

('Is that subjunctive important?'
'Indispensable, Monsieur Gretz.')

'Well, dear colleagues, Napoleon was right. Through his spy-glass, General Kutuzov pointed out to his Emperor the breach on the other side of the three lakes – and take note of their names – Lakes Melnitz, Telnitz and Sastchau. *And, in this campaign which we are undertaking against those who would commit this crime against humanity, may the names of these three lakes shine like flashing signals in your brains, and when you see the enemy fall into one of the traps that you have laid for him, savour your victory to the fullest, even to the point of saying to yourselves and amongst yourselves – did you see them when they rode out onto the Sastchau?'*

('With the purest of German accents?')

'I should like to quote for you,' Lord-Qui-Rote went on, 'the very words of Napoleon's soldiers as they fired upon the troops of the Czar Alexander and saw them fall – imagining as they did so all the widows, wives and mistresses who were to lament the news that a handsome husband or lover had been cut down on the field of Austerlitz. They said to each other: *We're going to cause a lot of tears to flow among the little ladies of Saint Petersburg.* And may I too, deep inside, hear you speak those same words when you feel at last that we are overcoming those who stand against us. When the elderly start to be afraid of losing their old-age pensions, and when everybody begins to think that the day is close at hand when the world will come to an end.'

'But on the field of Austerlitz, what happened?' Lord-Qui-Pète-Et-Qui-Rote shouted suddenly in his nasal voice, as if to shake us out of our waking dreams. 'The Czar having authorized it, General Kutuzov did indeed send his men out onto the three lakes, in a cloud of snow kicked up by the horses. Then, listen to this, this is the important part, Napoleon gave orders that his cannoneers lob their cannon balls onto the ice in order that it might break, thereby drowning the Russian cavalry.'

'However,' the Prime Minister went on, 'the cannoneers discovered that the ice of the three lakes was too thick and that their cannon balls were bouncing off it. But what were the names of the three lakes? Is there anyone in this room who can tell me that *instanter* and on the spot?'

He asked the question in a state of great agitation.

'Telnitz, Melnitz and Sastchau,' answered one of his pee-wees.

'That's it exactly. Bravo, dear colleague, you in particular will go far.'

This was said like a veiled threat to each of the others.

'So then what did Napoleon's cannoneers immediately do, upon the orders of their beloved Little Corporal? They pointed the muzzles of their guns towards the sky so that the balls would fall from higher up, thus multiplying their weight by π (3.1416) of their mass, according to the celebrated law of Lord Acton. No, I beg your pardon, I mean Isaac Newton, and the law that he discovered when he was hit on the nose by an apple falling from a tree.'

('Another of the fruits of his universal wisdom.')

'Next point, dear friends. Have I spoken to you concerning Menier chocolate and its beneficial effect upon the brain?'

Chapter Thirteen

The Commission

'The Commission now requests the presence of the witness Albert d'Adalbert, alias George-Esteem de Dunberry,' thundered the voice of the president of the Permanent Commission above the heads of the mixed bag of curiosity-seekers who were massed that morning in the Checkered Salon and whose numbers surpassed even those of the members of Parliament, the ex-ministers, the journalists and the ex-journalists, all forming a huge crowd drawn slavering by rumours of a day of blood-letting at Parliament. Because the day's witnesses were no small fry but rather key witnesses and the ones who might finally be able to unlock the strong-box of truth.

Slouching at ease in one of the sticky red leatherette couches of the Checkered Salon, Gerry Gretz was installed face to face with his usual informant, the member from the riding of Mes Deux.* Thus, he was to the right of the president and behind the government members.

'What post did you occupy at the time of the events to be examined by this parliamentary commission, Monsieur de Dunberry?' asked the president.

---

* 'Mes Deux' may be taken to mean 'Mes Deux Fesses', which would be translated as 'my two buttocks' or 'my arse' (Translator's note).

'I was Commissioner-in-Chief of the Royal Canadian Horseback Police, Monsieur le Président.'

'Are you therefore in a position to tell us who, in the middle of the night, drew up a list of five hundred innocent people who were then put under arrest and thrown into prison for no reason at all?'

The commissioner's lawyer, Maître Ange-Albert de Saint-Geoffroid interrupted.

'Objection, Monsieur le Président. My client, Albert d'Adalbert, has only just stepped out of a Koala Airlines Plane, the long-haul, non-stop flight from Sydney. He is still suffering the effects of what is known as jet and geography lag. So he would have difficulty giving a point-blank answer to that question which lies at the very heart of the labours of this commission, since your mandate, Monsieur le Président, is precisely to determine if the said list was drawn up in conformity with the laws of the country or as the result of an abuse of power by the executive.'

'I believe that in this particular instance,' said the member for Mes Deux, 'it would have been more appropriate, instead of *point-blank*, to say *point-scarlet*, since all over this wide world, the Royal Canadian Horseback Police are known, and known equally well to the kangooroos of Australia as to the unfortunate Indians who have been deprived of their lands right here, by the expression *red-shirts*.'

'The member for Mes Deux is absolutely right,' interjected the police witness.

The president, who couldn't put up with very much of this, turned authoritatively to the witness.

'In the first place, Monsieur, even though you may have been commissioner, here you are not allowed to take the floor until I give you permission – unless your long sojourn among the koalas has fostered some new concept of etiquette or, more specifically, of parliamentary procedure?'

It was Maître Saint-Geoffroid who answered. He certainly knew the procedure, descending as he did from one of the most illustrious families of the bench in all this unhappy land. He had, moreover, gone to university during the same years as Lord-Qui-Pète-Et-Qui-Rote-Dans-le-Trou-d'Eau, himself descended from the no less celebrated Don-Qui-Rote-de-la-Mancha.

'My client is chewing his fingernails in mortification already,' he said.

'I am still speaking, Maître,' said the president. 'And to the member for Mes Deux, that warning goes for you too. Besides, it's not *goo*, it's *ga*.'

'What do you mean, *ga* not *goo*?'

'You don't say kan*goo*roo, but rather kan*ga*roo, unless of course you happen to be speaking French,' said the president. 'But you still have the floor, Maître de Saint-Geoffroid.'

'With heartfelt gratitude, Monsieur le Président, I am behooved to take it forthwith.'

'Not *are* behooved, but it behooves *you*, Maître,' insisted the president.

'Behooved, behooves, I'm afraid I don't understand, Monsieur le Président.'

'One is not behooved, but rather it behooves one to do something, my dear Maître. But never mind, just keep on hooving along.'

'Before going on to the testimony of my client, may I humbly request of this commission that we adjourn the sitting until tomorrow at fourteen hundred hours?'

'No problem, if the two parties here represented are in agreement, naturally.'

The next day at fourteen hundred hours the session opened with the testimony of a medical expert, Professor Lucien Grondines de Saint-Molaires, son and grandson of famous dentists.

'In their case,' Gerry thought to himself, 'we shouldn't really say dentists, but orthodontists.'

Then the member for Mes Deux took the initiative. 'Well,' he said, 'what enlightenment do you have for us upon this day?'

His choice of words gave the president another excuse.

'Ah, how I do admire your phraseology, *upon this day*, Monsieur le Député for Mes Deux! I almost envy the voters of Mes Deux for having you as their representative.'

But the member was not to be deflected.

'I presume that this has to do with the medical file of the witness Albert d'Adalbert,' he said.

'Right you are, Monsieur le Député,' said the orthodontist, 'that's the reason why I'se here.'

The president interrupted. 'It's not the reason *why*, but the reason *for which*, dear Doctor. And we don't say *I'se* but *I'm*.'

'Yer the boss, Your Honour. That's the reason whime I'm here. Your witness, Albert d'Adalbert, alias George-Esteem de Dunberry, has been under my care for many moons gentlemen, and besides that it was on my advice that he left our so inhospitable country.'

'I beg your pardon?' asked the president.

'Eight windshields smashed in three weeks, Monsieur le Président,' said the medical expert, 'gives a man something to worry about.'

'I agree, I do agree Doctor, but I find it difficult to countenance hearing you speak ill of my country.'

But the doc went on.

'You know,' he said, 'in the business practised by my client, you don't make only friends, and when retirement time comes along it's usually best to go and suntan one's family jewels somewhere else.'

'We must shorten the proceedings,' said the president, '*tempus fugit* and already evening begins to cast upon us its sombre mantle of darkness.'

'Awright, lady and gentlemen members, this is what it's about. This is an extremely rare disease of which I am the discoverer and which has earned me the title of Comrade in Medicine from the University of Moscow, a title which I accepted even if, as I admitted to them, I would never vote for them. And this disease I have baptized *neurogryphosis*, a word which comes half from Latin and half from Greek. However, not to wander into etymology, which is not what this commission is interested in. Let us rather discuss the symptoms of this terrible malady. What happens in fact? Because this is a disease which ravages the brains of people who work too hard. And what happens in the brains of people who have fallen victim to neurogryphosis is as follows – the sufferer's neurons dry out and become as hard and brittle as claws.

'Whence the name of the disease.'

'As usual, Monsieur le Président, you've caught on right away. But to get back to my neurons. Instead of contacting with each other....'

'Or *making* contact....'

'Or *making* contact, now what would you mean by that, Monsieur le Président?'

'Not contacting with each other, but *making contact with* each other... the word *contact* is a noun, not a verb.'

'Right. So, instead of the ones making it with the others, as your president would put it, through the agency of what are called scientifically the synapses, the neurons ignore each other – or ignore with each other – a question of style, Monsieur le Président. They refuse to collaborate and to carry out the orders issued to them by their owner. To make it short, and to get to the question that you are concerned about, when a person like my client and your witness is stricken with this malady, he's up against the cunning obstinacy of his neurons. His neurons are laughing at him. You might even say that the afore-mentioned neurons take a wicked delight in frustrating the commands issued by the brain. For example the victim may burst out laughing at the most inappropriate moments, such as when he kneels at the tomb of a dead person. And therefore, should the witness suddenly burst out laughing for no apparent reason, do not hold it against him because he is in no way responsible. It's not my client laughing, it's his brain.'

The member for Mes Deux, brutal as always, summed it up for him.

'In other words, he doesn't remember a thing.'

'Not only does he not remember a thing,' said the expert witness, 'but his memory takes an evil pleasure in concealing precisely the things that you want to know.'

'So that what we have before us, Docteur de Saint-Molaires, is a case of selective neurogryphosis?'

'Exactly, Your Honour the Member for Mes Deux.'

'That's a big help, Monsieur le Président,' exclaimed the member. 'We pay for his trip back here from Sydney only to hear him tell us he's lost his memory.'

He muttered to himself – 'Go back to your bloody kangaroos, you goddamn Mountie'– but loud enough for the mechanical stenographer from Hansard to catch it – as well as his old comrade-in-arms Gerry Gretz, just in time for the next day's edition.

'Before I return to the antipodes, Monsieur le Président,' asked the neurogryphotic witness, 'would you allocate me the floor just one last time?'

'*Allow* me.'

'Thanks, Monsieur le Président.'

'No, no, no, Monsieur. I didn't mean allow me for me, I meant allow me for you. You should have asked me to *allow* you to speak, not to *allocate* you the floor.'

'So I can speak?'

'But yes, speak, speak,' said the president.

'Why not squeak, squeak, Monsieur le Président?' said the member for Mes Deux.

'You again? My dear Monsieur le Député, you have the biggest mouth....'

The witness was encouraged by this exchange.

'Okay, so I can speak now?'

'Yes, yes, go ahead.'

'So why'd you interrupt' me?

'...*rupt,*' said the president.

'Right, so I can talk now?'

'Of course, of course,' said the president. 'Go ahead and let's get it over with.'

'You will have noticed that I also bear the name of Georges-Esteem de Dunberry, which is my *nom de guerre* and very useful indeed for helping me to stand off attacks from all sorts of dangerous and undesirable characters. May I add that when I was baptized, for I am in fact an R.C., I was given the name of Georges-Estienne. A French name, gentlemen. Which serves to show that I couldn't possibly harbour any hostile sentiments as regards your collectivity and its so distinct French specificity.'

And then, believe it or not but the witness was shaken from head to foot with an uncontrollable fit of laughter.

'What did I tell you, lady and gentlemen members of Parliament? A classic attack of neurogryphosis.'

'In that case, with beautiful name like Georges-Estienne, would you had kept it to this day...,' said the member for *Mes Deux*.

'Ah, that subjunctive is music to my ears,' murmured the president.

The witness was once again perfectly calm and said, 'I was expecting you to ask me why I didn't. My parents had enrolled me at Maggie University, venerated for its tolerance and its respect for minorities. They'll even consent to speak French to you there, if you insist and if you've only just learned it. And in those high places of the mind and the spirit and general knowledge, my literature professor, who was also my girlfriend, suggested that I might do well to adopt an English given name if I wanted to spare myself some impossible questions at the oral exam and certain failure.'

'I see,' said the president, 'and if it's not indiscreet, may I ask what was the subject of your thesis?'

The member for Mes Deux objected.

'I fail to see the relevancy of your question, Monsieur le Président, and I refer you to the rules.'

This despite howls of protest from the mob of curiosity-seekers who wanted to hear the answer.

'Silence in the room,' shouted the president, 'or I'll have it cleared. I am obliged to turn my attention to the question of rules which has been raised by the member for Mes Deux. I'm supposed to render a decision on the spot regarding my own question to the witness. Imagine my torment as a judge and a participant.'

'Next witness,' called the opposition member.

'Not before I've rendered my decision, Monsieur le Député. The judge still has certain rights. And now I'm prepared to render that decision. By virtue of the Cacanada Bill, I am allowed to ask my question because the preamble of the afore-mentioned Bill affirms that minorities have rights. So, since I am in the minority here, being the only president, I'm asking it. What was the subject of your thesis?'

'It was this, Monsieur le Président. Did the Gurkhas deserve their status as genuine English subjects because of India's attachment to the British Empire, or because they fired on their fellow Hindus during the battle of Roosevelt Downs – just as British soldiers would have done?'

The expert medical witness wanted to ask a question. 'Monsieur le Président, would you permit me to make an remark irregardless?'

'*Regardless*, Monsieur le Docteur.'

'What do you mean, Monsieur le Président?'

'We don't say *irregardless*, we say *regardless*.'

'Oh,' said the orthodontist. 'Well irregardless, I just wanted to point out to the commission another example of my witness's illness. He has perfect recall of the title of his thesis although it dates back forty years. This is a classic illustration of the effects of the disease. Proof by absurdity.'

'*Ex absurdo* or *a contrario?*' the member for Mes Deux wanted to know.

'Monsieur le Député,' the president declared abruptly, 'the Cacanada Bill permits the utilization of only one other language in Parliament, and it's not Latin.'

'If I would of known, I would of kept quiet,' said the member.

'If I *had* known,' said the president.

'If you'd of known what?'

'You're supposed to say *if I had known*, and not *if I would have known*, and never never *if I would of known*, because you need an auxiliary verb there and not a preposition. This is not just a whim of mine, even if I were unlucky enough to have whims. *Of* is a preposition.'

'A prepo... propo... a what?' asked the witness.

'Oh you who enter into this Parliament, abandon ye all grammatical concerns at the cloakroom,' said the president.

It was eighteen hundred hours. The session was adjourned until two thousand hours.

Chapter Fourteen

The Solicitor

Maître Joe de Figaro, friend of the famous Lord-Qui-Pète-Dans-le-Trou-d'Eau, was not born yesterday. Every evening he was to be seen in the girlie bars, in the process of soliciting himself one for the night. In his chosen field he had set records which remain unsurpassed to this day.

'Sometimes after a night of love, I still have to masturbate twice just to steady my nerves in the morning.'

Everyone was in awe of him, including his client and principal witness in this affair, who generally chose him as his solicitor in cases which no one else would have solicited.

'I'm listening, Maître,' said the witness, 'and I am entirely at your disposal. But first, just to lighten things up a bit, tell me all about your latest escapade.'

'Well, she's got the biggest boobs in town, Monsieur. I'd had my eye on her for months but every time I tried to talk to her, some goof would interrupt and spoil everything, so I never got the chance to sample her wares. Then last night I had a stroke of luck, she was on her own. She was dancing in the middle of the floor, waving her arms like an oil derrick in the desert. She recognized me by my dark glasses and she spoke to me.'

'Hi Joe, want to dance?'

'Yes, I said, and her beautiful boobs bounced up and down to the same rhythm as the derrick. I got more and more turned on. In fact I've come here straight from her bed, Your Excellency.'

'And she told you that no one before you had ever given her such a fantastic orgasm.'

'Who told you that?'

'Just guessing, my friend, just guessing. I was young once too.'

'Yes, indeed, Your Excellency, and not even flush enough to drive them home. They've been seen on the doorstep of your modest residence, hailing taxis at seven in the morning.'

'Well, what do you expect? That's the time when I do my body-building and my body-building is sacred. It's the exercice of kings. However, let's get down to brass tacks. You've been designated to question me about the five hundred arrests?'

'By yourself, Your Excellency....'

'Then let's proceed.'

'On what legal or historical precedent did you base your decision to arrest five hundred innocent people in the middle of the night, just like that, and in flagrant contravention of their rights?'

'First of all, because I knew most of them. They were friends, or almost. So I can assure you that I had nothing against them personally. Now, however, they all realize that when my duty to the security of the state demands it, I shall not hesitate to draw my sword. It was Marchament Nedham who said, in the time of Cromwell – and make sure you get this down, stenographer – he said, *Would God confer strength upon the unworthy?*'

'Certainly,' said Maître de Figaro. 'Just like my prick, when it feels the urge nothing can stand in its way and I make it my sceptre.'

'Better than spectre, as Willy the Bard would have said....'

'And sovereignty,' added the witness, 'is more usually found on the side of those who possess the Lee-Enfields than on the side of those who have only hay-forks, manure-shovels, scythes and sap-dippers.'

'Please note that, stenographer. Sovereignty is a Lee-Enfield.'

'King Charles the First once opposed that.'

'True,' said the swordsman, 'but there came a day when all his edicts and orders fell silent!'

'And when was that?'

'When they chopped off his head. Long before the petty pretentious French did it to Louis XVI, two centuries further along. Tell the newspapers that those five hundred prisoners who're complaining about me should be proud to be the spiritual descendants of Lilburne, Overton Walwyn and Thomas Prince. The only difference was that instead of the Tower of London, their dungeon was what they so prettily styled the Parthenais Hilton.'

'Why are you so set against them?'

'For two reasons, you skirt-chasing little pettifogger. The first is that if ever they were to get what they want, then the power of the army and of the Church, all the weight, the leverage, the guillotine, would fall into the hands of a bunch of unprincipled plebians, nobodies, or, to return once more to the words of my preceptor, Marchament Nedham, *to the dregs of society, persons who are nobody, who are nothing, who own no property and who despise those who do. From them, we could expect only the worst – licentiousness, confusion and anarchy.*'

'For example...?'

'Well, they could throw five hundred innocent people into jail at any time, just like that, in the middle of the night or whenever they felt like it and for no reason.'

'So have you seen the list of names?'

'By all means, yes, I've seen the list. Had some good chuckles over it too. A bunch of penniless strivers, a scribbling writer or two, quite a few ambitious scramblers and pretentious *poseurs* plus a number of red-arsed climbing types.* There were even some I personally crossed off because I knew they'd be preening themselves over it for the rest of their lives. But I left most of them. And I added some too, just

---

* 'Les rouges': The Liberals (Translator's note).

to see if they could scrape up the funds to outlast me and carry on. Against wind and tide and adversity.'

'And the second?'

'The second what?'

'The second reason for going after them so doggedly.'

The witness remembered that he'd been giving reasons.

'The second reason was that I hate Balkanization.'

'Yes, and....'

'I am bitterly disappointed. Because no one even holds it against me any more. I have been forgiven. I'm nothing now but a dead leaf drifting along the sands of the shore, waiting to be carried off by the first gust of wind. Ah life, life... my dear Joe!'

'What's wrong with life?'

'Is it worth living? But there you have it my dear chap, I've finished. Have you got enough? Because I'm busy now, this is the time of day when I swim my twenty lengths and with me that's sacred. So, thanks a lot and have a nice day, I hope things keep on jumping for you. See you at the next War Measures Act, you little fucker. And say hello for me to the nice big boobs if you see her again. I think I may have crossed swords with her myself when I was younger.'

'Very well then, I'll take my leave of you, Your Excellency. Please forgive me for having been so brutal with you, but that was my mandate from the National Assembly.'

'That's true, I was forgetting. If by any chance I should have to appear in court, try to choose a date when Tonio Mémère is on the bench. He owes me for lots of things.'

'Agreed.'

Chapter Fifteen

Dragana

When Wolfrid Milton and his wife Doomsday gave birth to their daughter Dragana, they made Dolorosa a grandmother and from that day on her life was transformed. It was as if at last love had come to her and as if, above all, she had found someone to whom she could offer her own love. She smothered Dragana with it wall-to-wall. And she did battle with Wolfrid and Doomsday to have the little girl with her as often and as long as possible. She took to telling Wolfrid bare-faced lies about the ease with which the baby would fall asleep at her house, and the number of hours in the night that she would sleep straight through. Wolfrid couldn't believe his ears.

'You must have a lenitive effect on our baby girl.'

'Lenitive? I don't like the sound of that,' said Dolorosa. 'Sounds too much like Lenin.'

You would have thought that Dolorosa had been saving up her love forever, waiting for the moment when little Dragana would appear in this world to reveal to her her grand passion. Each second of Dragana's life was a marvel to her. She kept an album whose every page commemorated some event in the child's life.

On the first page there was her little footprint, and then a lock of blond hair (but not wheat blond, enough of wheat and wheat blond....)

Things reached a point where, one day, Wolfrid complained.

'You don't love me any more Dolorès, there's no room left in your heart for anyone but Dragana. I feel like an orphan.'

He and his wife were sure that sooner or later Dolorosa was going to kidnap the little girl and they had all their locks changed. One day Gretz found Dolorosa in tears, her shoulders heaving with violent sobs.

'They want to take Dragana away from me,' she said. 'Doomsday says I'm bringing her up all wrong. She doesn't think it's normal for her to sleep at my place so much of the time and so little at home. So, it's all over, I've lost her, they won't let me have her any more.'

'Oh, no, no, no,' said Gerry, reassuring her. 'As soon as they have trouble finding a babysitter, they'll bring her right back to you, don't worry.'

And sure enough, the very next morning Wolfrid brought Dragana back to Dolorosa's place for two days. When he opened the door, a tidal wave of love nearly washed him and the baby back down the stairs. Two days later, when he returned to pick up his little daughter, Wolfrid asked his mother about her obsession.

'But you love her much too much. It isn't normal. It's as if you'd never loved anyone else in all your life.'

'Listen, Wolfrid my dear. In my life, I've had only one great love. He was a little no-good nothing-at-all named Gerry Gretz. But he was everything to me – husband, son, brother, father and grandfather. It was no accident that I called him my Pope. I listened to him for days on end. It was almost a secret, the way we used to see each other, like a pair of lovers. We'd both get up at the break of day, before anyone else in the house was moving. And we'd talk about our lives, the day that had finished and the day that was just beginning. Our joys, our sufferings, the reasons we had to be happy or unhappy, why we wanted to go on living or why we thought of giving up. I lived through him. A child lives ten times more intensely than a grown-up. Everything that happens to a child is happening to him for the first time. When he cries, he cries with every pore of his skin, with every alveole of his lungs and with every neuron of his brain, because he's all one. Do you know what it means to be all one? And now it's little Dragana. She's my next Pope. The first female Pope!'

Even the candy display in the store was beginning to suffer as a result of Dolorosa's fixation. All re-arranging and re-organization of the display window had come to an end. Dolorosa just did not care.

When Dragana reached the age of twenty-five, the same undiminished love continued to reign between her and her grandmother. They had become confidantes. Dragana told her grandmother everything. Her problems at school, her problems in love, it all came out – the first troubling, meaningful glances to have been sent her way, the first heart-throbs, the first deep feelings and the first decisions. She had even talked about her work for Wolfrid and, just recently, about her meeting with Gerry Gretz.

'Not my Pope...?' asked Dolorosa.

'The very same. Your Pope is an extremely special person. He's the first man to have given more thought to my pleasure than to his own.'

'He had a good start in life,' said Dolorosa, proudly.

'Why, did you go to bed with him, Grandmaw?'

'Are you crazy, sweetie? There was a forty-year age difference between us. There was never any question of that. But time was when Gerry used to come and tell me everything, just as you do now.'

Chapter Sixteen

Scaloppini's Hockey Pool

'Gretz my friend, I'm asking you not to kick me when I'm down. Because I'm at a loss to tell you straight out and without beating around the bush (not bushes, but bush) what my men have discovered and even more at a loss to tell you what I make of it all.'

'Never mind, let's begin at the end. What do you make of it all?'

'Madame Dolorosa had Marcotte, first name Mario, by the balls.'

'Some people would say she had him by the *chenolles*.'

'Well that's just my problem. I hardly know what to call the things any more. If there's one anatomical part under the sun that keeps changing its name, that's it. In the medical dictionary it's easy, they're testicles, otherwise called bags. But if you look in the *Pierre Guiraud*, or the *Eric Partridge*, or the *Xenopoulos*, the word has so many variants that you could say about it what La Fontaine said about the female sex:

*Bien souvent il varie, bien fol qui s'y fie.**

---

* 'Very often they change, and very mad is he who trusts them (Translator's note).'

'All that counts, dear Inspector, is that we understand each other, so let's agree on *chenolles*.'

'Okay, we'll say *chenolles*. Nobody knows where that one comes from, not even Léandre Bergeron has anything to say about it.'

'Before asking you what difference that makes, I suppose I should ask you just how she had him by the *chenolles*.'

'Yes, my friend, and before asking me exactly how she had him, you should ask me how we found out.'

'Okay, Kirié Kolo, how did you find out?'

'There was a secret hiding place in Madame Bouillé's store and in there Madame Dolorosa kept all that was most precious to her, like old cigar boxes from brands that vanished long ago, Sir Wilfred Laurier for example. And in one of those boxes we found a bundle of bills from Scaloppini's hockey pool. You remember that? The pool where you had to guess the exact time of the last goal scored in a hockey game at the Forum?'

'I'd forgotten about the pool, but I can still see Jean Béliveau standing up in the penalty box and pointing to the clock in the Forum because it'd skipped a second.'

'That's just it. It had skipped at eighteen minutes and thirty-two seconds. And all the tickets sold by Scaloppini were marked with exactly that time. So, naturally, there couldn't be a winner, except for Scaloppini himself and he collected tens of thousands of Dominion of Canada dollars after every game.'

'What it comes down to is that Mother Dolorosa was working Mario Marcotte's territory, retailing tickets for the pool.'

'*Crisse* but you catch on quick.'

'I may not be Greek but I did go to school.'

'However, with all due respect, what does that prove?'

'Well, just that she could call the tune to make Mario dance.'

'Dance maybe, I'm delighted to hear it, but now will he sing?'

'Yes, of course, as soon as he gets his memory back.'

'To change the subject,' said Kolo, 'and return to the subject of *chenolles*, do you know the one about the Blacks in Mississippi?'

'No, but it'd better be good.'

'A Black from Mississippi, named Titus Oatmeal, got a subpoena from the police. He asked his father what a subpoena was and his father told him that *sub* comes from underneath and that *poena* comes from penis. It means they've got you by the balls, is what he said.'

'Do I have your permission to repeat that story to others?' asked Gretz.

'By all means,' said Kolokotronis. 'Go forth and repeat yourself and multiply.'

'She must have used him to get rid of Sylvio Debs. But Debs's death was a straight accident, that's in your report.'

'My dear Gretz, you are forgetting that the ways of the Lord are unknowable.'

'My God how true that is....'

Chapter Seventeen

The Funeral

Everyone wanted to get his name or his face into the paper so that he could say to his descendants that he was there, at the Funeral, when the Personage was buried. Therefore anything inside the church or anywhere near it that looked even remotely like a reporter or any kind of pencil-pusher was treated with exceptional consideration. It was assumed by most of those present that if you wanted to get your name into the paper, you had to cough up. For a Montreal paper, the price was ten dollars. For the regional rags, things like the *A-1 Hebdomadaire de Rapièreville,* where Gerry Gretz was working at the time, the price fell to five dollars.

The Great Man's whole stable was in attendance: entrepreneurs, organizers, guys who had been put into office just to keep the seat warm in the National Assembly, guys who had kindly organized themselves to vote for people who were out of town, guys who marshalled the *claques* for meetings and guys who arranged for the dead to vote; judges from the Supreme Court and others who hoped to become judges, senators and hopefuls who wanted to become senators, not forgetting the recipients of radio station permits and the recipients of television station permits. Everyone who'd ever made a buck thanks to the Great Man, either in the past or in the present. The scientific survey agencies were there, the film-makers and the suck-up pseudo film-makers, the wives who'd had part-time jobs during the campaign, the boot-polishers from the university, and the tormented souls who always suffered the right torments at the right time. There were those who had even stuck up for the army and the police when it looked like a good thing to do, and those who'd accepted free furniture and who hadn't even realized it until the police enquiry came along. *Oh, so that was a gift, was it, well what do you think of that...? If only I'd known...!* There were also the Crown lawyers who, at the right time, had forgotten to ask the right questions. There were the desk editors who'd retouched photographs for the front page, the double agents who'd infiltrated the unions, the radicals who disappeared every six months, the *bourgeoises* in mink coats who terrorized little old ladies in cloth coats, the types who betrayed for credit and sold themselves for cash, and the intellectuals who always waited to see which way the rain was blowing before opening their umbrellas. The little church in Rapièreville was full to overflowing. There were people standing in the aisles and climbing up on the steel-toed Kodiaks of the guys behind them. Some of them were wetting their combs in the holy water. Some of the faithful were sitting in the confessionals. Others had climbed onto chairs. Some had even climbed into the *crèche*, disguised as Mary and Joseph in order to get closer to the cold body of the Great Man. And from the wide-open doors of the church, right up to the altar rail, the heavies from the federal police force were lined up like fence posts along both sides of the centre aisle.

'There are two kinds of men in politics,' said Cardinal Thing-a-Majig, who sounded as if he were reading an article from *Maclean's Magazine*. 'There are those who, gifted with superior intellect, can simultaneously keep aloft concepts of law, philosophy and history with all the skill of a circus juggler. There are others who know that elections are not to be won with prayer and who manipulate consciences, buying and selling them and throwing them out after use like Bic razors. And once in a very long while there appears among us an exceptional individual who displays a capacity for both of these talents. The Elite Personage whom the Creator has today called home to himself was one of those exceptional beings who appear only once or twice in a generation or in a century. That so small a nation as ours, as he himself would have put it, should produce such a specimen, is nothing short of a miracle. He regularly attended services at this modest country church because here he was better able to speak to his God than in the sumptuous cathedrals of our cities. And thus it is that I can still see him before me, closer no doubt than many of you ever did, just as I saw him on all those countless occasions when I laid the Host upon his tongue. Ah, such a face! He had deep lines, Grand Canyons in his face, that showed better than anything else his force of concentration and his peerless capacity for thought. From here to the South Pole, there was no problem he had not agonized over. How many nights, how many hours, must he have spent in reflection – that is, when the unhappy creatures whom he frequented for purely hygienic reasons left him the time – and how even that shows nonetheless that he was human too, only human.'

'And that face! No other man of politics from his generation could smile as he did, as magically and mysteriously as the Mona Lisa. And, I might add, what eternal vitality in a face still marked with the acne of his teen-aged years, the marks above all of his youthfulness of mind and of heart. What a face! What a symbol! What a man! Let us imagine him on high, sitting between the Holy Trinity and the Seraphim and let us envy God, or almost, for having received him at last into His bosom. What conversations the two of them must be having about the meaning of life and about the country, such happiness!'

Out front on the steps, latecomers were wandering around with ten-dollar bills in their hands, chasing after journalists. One of them came up to Gerry Gretz and asked him what paper he wrote for.

'Where do you want to get your name in, my dear sir?'

'Into the big fat one, *La Presse*,' answered the mourner.

'Lucky for you,' said Gerry, 'that just happens to be the paper I work for. How much are you prepared to pay to get your name in?'

'At least fifteen dollars,' said the man in black.

'I can do it for you for twenty,' said Gerry.

'Done,' said the entrepreneur and added, 'just to make sure there aren't any typographical errors in my name, here's a pen with my company's slogan on it. Everything's there, even my postal code.'

'P.A. Des Groseilliers, Cranes and Heavy Machinery,' said the ballpoint.

'Thanks twenty times over,' said Gretz. 'It'll be in tomorrow, the first edition, don't miss it.'

'Never in a hundred years,' said P.A.

The weather reports kept saying that that day in Rapièreville was the hottest on record. Through the town the rumour ran like wildfire: *The gates of hell are open.*

The service was almost over. From the back of the church, Gerry Gretz called out the first verse like a psalmody.

'He was our Prime Minister....'

And the congregation, in perfect unison, intoned the response.

'Lord, have mercy upon us....'

'He wanted the best for us.'

'Lord, have mercy.'

'He drew up a charter for *ein tausend Jahre.*'

'Seigneur, ayez pitié de nous.'

'He loved his people.'

'Lord, have mercy....'

Cardinal Newman was wriggling on his chair, very much as if his bladder were tormenting him. His pretty little patent leather pumps, magenta in colour and with silver buckles, were torturing his feet. He couldn't hold still.

'He loved a *demoiselle.*'

'Lord, have mercy on poor her....'

And, in a sonorous voice, Gretz finished with a quotation from François Villon.

'And pray God will consent to absolve him.'

A heartfelt *amen* rolled through the nave. The cardinal stood up and took things in hand again.

'Sufficit,' he said. 'This is a matter for our mother the Holy Church and not a time for a settling of accounts with the past.'

'Ite, missa est.'

And in two seconds flat, everybody in the church was out on the steps yakking.

Some of them had kept the Host in the corners of their mouths and now plucked it delicately out to press between the pages of their prayer books as a souvenir.

'I remember the time he pinched my cheek between his index and middle fingers....'

'I remember the time he butted out a cigarette on my forehead....'

'I remember the time he told me to go shit.'

After the good townsfolk, there came the special guests. Toto and Titi were there, and Blondie and Dagwood. Also the Phantom, Maggie and Jiggs, Jacques le Matamore, L'il Abner, Petunia and Popeye, Dick Tracy, and Dennis the Menace with Marmaduke. The special envoy from the President of the United States was the little Mexican with the perfect teeth who used to advertise Dentyne gum. Diane was there too with Cheetah, her she-monkey, clutched firmly to her hip. The mayor's wife of Rapièreville decided that Cheetah's exposed gums, as she pulled back her lips in a monkey rictus, were indecent. Nor did she trouble to conceal from Diane her feelings about letting that animal smile *on this dark day for humanity.*

'But she's not smiling, it's a tic,' said Diane.

'All you had to do was not bring her here....' The mayor's lady was almost screaming, jolting the faithful out of their contemplation.

'But she was so fond of the departed....'

Only Cardinal Newman succeeded in restoring some semblance of order on the steps of the church. He gave Cheetah a good smack in the face which produced the desired effect. She pulled her lips back down over her gums.

Chapter Eighteen

The Crucifix

The funeral procession set off down the central pathway through the cemetery. The grave had been dug into the soft sandy yellow soil of the first escarpment above Rapièreville and the pile of sand was hidden under a green imitation grass carpet. Stretched over the grave were three straps which were part of the latest contraption for letting down the coffin. The oak coffin itself was installed in the centre and the president of Les Pompes Funèbres Enregistrées (who was an important member of the Party) was champing with impatience at the prospect of trying out his new system for the first time. He'd been saving it for just some special occasion such as this. In the cemetery, there wasn't a dry eye. Not a handkerchief that wasn't out. And every handkerchief had its particular personality – here a blue one with white polka-dots on it and there, in the hairy hand of a bodyguard, a little white one with beehives. There was the timid handkerchief of the person who keeps it balled up in his fist and pulls out just a tiny corner that he hopes is the cleanest part and there were the endless white handkerchiefs of the pacifists.

When the coffin was properly settled in the middle of the straps, Cardinal Thing-a-Majig stepped up to the grave and pronounced a few words in the dead man's two languages.

'Ashes to ashes,' he said, 'and dust to dust. *Seigneur, tu as rappelé à toi ton serviteur*, the Great Man, the Personage, thereby depriving us all of his guidance and his inspiration. In your almighty power, Lord, have a thought for us – and if the Las Vegas Comic from the other side wants to reopen the debate one more time, when the majority has already voted, once and for all, cleanly and honestly and aboveboard, its adherence to the proper forms – then do not hesitate, Lord, to come to our aid once more, reminding us incessantly that victories are not won by Providence but by well-greased Lee-Enfields, good dry ammunition and plenty of it, numerical superiority in troops, all the millions we could wish for and love of God and Country. Let us pray God and keep our powder dry.'

Then at a sign from Cardinal Peter C. Thing-a-Majig, the president of Les Pompes Funèbres Enregistrées at last got to put his foot on the remote control starter of his coffin-lowering mechanism and the contraption purred softly into action. But the coffin had descended only a few inches when, with a peremptory gesture, the cardinal stopped the operation and turned to the family.

'Would anyone like to keep the crucifix?'

The widow felt obliged to say yes. The president reached into the pockets of his striped trousers and produced a handsome new screwdriver, the latest thing, with a full selection of points screwed into its handle – Phillips, Robertson, X-shaped, regular and whatever else there is. He held it out to the cardinal with exactly the respectful alacrity of a nurse handing the surgeon a lancet and the cardinal set about unscrewing the crucifix. But his magenta skullcap had an embarrassing tendency to slide forward on his brilliantined hair and down onto the Florida tan on his handsome forehead. So he had to keep pushing it back. And he was distinctly heard to say: 'Goddamned skull-cap....'

When he had got the first screw out, he gave it to Madame and the widow slipped it into her pocket. After the third screw, he gingerly lifted the crucifix from the coffin, touching it with just the tips of his fingers as if it were white-hot. The widow then opened her handbag a crack and he dropped it in.

A human tide had washed up around the grave. As the oak coffin started down again into the hole, the crowd began to sing in chorus:

> *I'll see him again one day,*
> *I'll see him again one day*
> *In his homeland in Heaven,*
> *In his homeland in Heaven.*

But they had not counted on the guys from Lapalme, for whom Gerry Gretz had made up a little ditty which was somewhat more profane:

> *When I see you again*
> *small, medium or large*
> *Guerletons glin-glon*
> *It'll be in Hell, you bastard.*

It didn't take long before the cops from the R.Cee.M.Pee., who weren't much into folksinging, decided to put an end to the concert. They grabbed Gerry Gretz by the arms and legs, swung him like a sack of laundry and tossed him into the back of the local paddy wagon. As he landed, Gerry felt two contradictory sensations on his forehead, first the warmth of the blood trickling from his scalp and then the cold steel floor of the truck.

'You beat me and you club me and I don't give a fuck, you kick me and knock me down and keep on kicking me and I don't give a fuck, you pick me up by the arms and legs and throw me hard into the back of your truck, into drunk's piss and whore's puke, and I don't give a fuck, because I'll never give in. For the goons from the R.Cee.M.Pee., I have nothing but loathing. And as for the *not on his grave* I give less than a fuck, and for the reproaches of *badly brought up* and *bad mannered* and *foul-mouthed* and *no education* and *it isn't done* and *my God how could he*, I use it all for bum-wipe. And the toadies sing about liberty. All their lives. Well, you can dump on me all you want, you can talk till you're tired. Because the more you react, the further we'll go and the madder you get the funnier we'll think it is. The angrier you are the more I'll laugh, and the more you threaten the more it turns me on, and the more you want me to feel guilty the more I'll tell you to go eat a carload of shit, is that clear enough?'

The following day in municipal court, Gerry Gretz, of no known address, was charged with disturbing the peace. The peace of the vast cemeteries lying out there in the light of the moon. When they let him out on bail, he took the time to go back up to the graveyard.

All the flowers on the funeral wreaths had dried and shrivelled. The earth over the grave of the Personage had been raked out flat and already sod had been laid over the place of interment. On the dead man's tall pink granite tombstone he read:

Here I am
Here I stay.

Chapter Nineteen

The Morgue

The beautiful girl at the switchboard called down the length of the newsroom to him.

'Gerry, telephone for you, it's a cop.'

'Kirié Gretz here....'

'Mind-reader, who told you it was me?'

'It was the gorgeous Michelle, she said it was a cop on the phone.'

'Cop or no cop, I may have the answer to your questions about Gri-Gri.'

'Where the devil are you?'

'I'm at the municipal police morgue, next door to the French restaurant.'

'The place where they serve them up cold?'

'That's it exactly. I'll wait for you.'

The municipal police called their morgue the Institut Médico-Légal. It was in the basement. First door past the Coke machine, the girl upstairs had told him.

To the left of the door there was a handsome, high-quality black plastic plaque with the words *Institut Médico-Légal* incised on it in clean white grooves. But in homage to the political movement of the day, some civil servant had taken a pencil and blacked in most parts of the letters on the plaque, leaving only the following message: *...stic...k i01*. Gretz walked in without knocking. Everything inside was the same dazzling white as the stick 101. The floor and the walls were ceramic tile, with a row of stainless steel tables, what the French from France call *inox*.

The inspector was planted in front of a cabinet with padlocked drawers. Only one of them was open, and pulled part way out. It was marked with the letter M.

The inspector opened the drawer and Gerry caught a glimpse of several press-to-close sandwich bags of the kind called Ziplocs. Attached to each of the bags was a cardboard tag with quite a lot of writing on it.

'You guys are really something,' said Gerry. 'So the cops use sandwich bags for storing the remains of the poor humans that we are.'

'You don't know much about public administration, old friend. *Primo*, baggies are cheaper than anything else we've ever used. *Deuzio*, they're transparent, so we can see the customer at a glance. And *tertio*, the whole department are now supplying themselves with baggies from the morgue. Me, for example. I've got three kids in the École Socrate and for three years now I haven't had to buy a single baggie from my Ishmaelite corner store.'

Very delicately, Gerry opened the bag and emptied its contents onto the steel table. There were ten or a dozen tiny pieces of filling, of a silvery colour. He held the baggie up to the harsh light of the fluorescent tubing on the ceiling and said to Kolo.

'Talk of a *tabarnacle*, it's her.'

'How can you be so sure?'

With his fingertips, Gerry extracted an object from the bag marked M and laid it on the table. It was a key-chain ornament in the form of a little golden apple.

'I was the one who gave her this, for her twenty-fourth birthday, it was supposed to look like her bottom. Is this all you've found?'

'Yes it is.'

'Can I keep one of her fillings?'

'You're supposed to call it an amalgam, it comes from the Arabic, *amal djamal*, and it means the carnal union of two bodies.'

'Are you giving me one, yes or no?'

'*Crisse*, are you crazy? Allowing a piece of evidence to take off like that? A dental curriculum is sacred proof. It's something all juries accept.'

'Yes, but I could testify too.'

'With what, that golden apple? Gri-Gri's buttocks? No serious juror would believe you.'

So, very carefully, Gerry put the pieces of his blown-up girlfriend back into the sandwich bag. Then he held it up to the light, softly touched his lips to the bag and said to it – *'Adieu, mon bel amour'*– before giving it back to Inspector Kolokotronis.

'Goddamn Milton, he'll pay for this. And it's not to the inspector that I'm saying that, it's to the friend. So let Stalin take that for an answer.'

Chapter Twenty

Electrocuted

'You do laminating?' Gerry asked the good-looking cashier.

'I can see you know how to read,' she said, 'it's only written in four-foot high Letraset in the front window.'

'And framing too?'

'Three-foot letters, same window,' said the girl, 'say, how old are you?'

'Forty-seven,' said Gerry. 'Why?'

'Because, in human males, eyesight begins to decline from the beginning of the forties. You confirm all the current studies. What do you want laminated?'

Out of his sow's ear wallet Gerry took a nice fresh clipping, its corners neatly squared, from the *Journal de Montréal*. The headline was set in Cooper black and spanned exactly two columns. It consisted of just one word:

ELECTROCUTED.

A citizen highly regarded in his neighbourhood lost his life yesterday while trying to enter his home by way of the balcony after having locked himself out. Not finding his keys in his pockets, he had borrowed a ladder from his neighbour to climb up to the second-floor balcony. In his haste, however, Wolfrid Milton touched a 14,400-volt Hydro-Québec line with the ladder. The only witness to the tragedy was Gustave Baedeker who tells us that Monsieur Milton was unable to let go of the ladder, being connected to it by an electrical current beyond his strength. The witness added that he flailed his arms and legs like an epileptic. Then he crashed to the ground, where the police found him when they arrived.

'Could you make me a photocopy of this clipping and then frame both of them for me?'

'Certainly, Monsieur. But you'll have to pay in advance.'

'Why?'

'There are just too many people who order things done and then never come and pick them up. I've got boxes full of the stuff.'

Chapter Twenty-One

Cooke and Sons

'Gentlemen and lady journalists. This is getting to be a habit. Second meeting with the press in less than six months. Should worry us all. Is our fair city going to the bad?'

'How should we know?' the police reporters responded in chorus.

'So what is it this morning?' said Inspector Kolokotronis, originally from Crete, and really asking the question of himself. 'Well, just let me tell you that, as that famed creator of fables, La Fontaine, would have put it, I'm completely floured. Dredged, befuddled and bamboozled. This case is beyond me, it says nothing to me at all, *nihil intéressant*.'

As always at these press conferences, the journalists present had delegated one of their number, a certain Gerry Gretz, to direct their questions to the inspector.

'First question,' said Gerry, 'and it's my own, Inspector, if you will allow me?'

'But of course, of course, let's hear it,' said Kolo, all honey.

'Is there some connection between this press conference we're having now and the one from a couple of months back, concerning the dear departed Sylvio Debs?'

'That's the question I've been asking myself, gentlemen and lady journalists, plural if you please, even if there's only one lady....'

'One what?' demanded Miss Josée-Anne.

'One *woman* journalist, dear lady,' said Kolo, who must have had a lecture from his boss. 'This situation is totally new to me. This many coincidences have got to be more than just chance.'

'What coincidences...?' shouted the chorus.

'First of all, the bomb in Ville Mont-Royal, placed under the nice little round bottom of a pretty girl with twelve amalgam fillings and a golden apple on her key-chain. After that, the execution of Sylvio Debs in his brick-red Duster, dead with his head on a pillow of fourteen thousand tomatoes from the Bank of Canada. This week it was the electric ladder for the much loved and respected Wolfrid Milton, a model neighbour who planted his tulip bulbs every spring and who never hesitated to use his twenty-two long rifle, as they call it in Paris and the suburbs, on all the dogs and sons of bitches who dug up his bulbs or his ivy, which were moreover very luxuriant, thanks to the jealous care he lavished on them. So, Monsieur Milton died on an electric ladder while trying to get into his place through a second-floor window. Up to that point, there's nothing unusual except that it's a damned painful way to die. Every year a good half-dozen old people die that way because of

Alzheimer's or Alvarez's diseases. Where things start to be very complicated is when we get to the fact that our department, which for months has been keeping an eye on Wolfrid Milton as part of a general investigation into Montreal's drug world, our department as I was saying, already knew that over the last few weeks Wolfrid Milton had gone through an excessive quantity of keys for his humble abode. This according to information obtained in the course of our enquiry from his suppliers, Henri Cooke and Sons, the best locksmiths in the whole province.'

'Because the late Wolfrid Milton was naturally suspicious. His doors were always double-bolted with deadlock bolts and security chains and the whole *toutim*....'

'What's the whole *toutim* mean?' In-Folio wanted to know.

'It's the whole *bataclan*, as we say in these parts, the whole kit'n'caboodle, the whole fling-flang.'

'Conclusion. There was probably someone close to Wolfrid Milton who was taking an evil and diabolical pleasure in causing his keys to vanish, thus wagering on Hydro-Québec. So here I have a victim on my hands, and the murder weapon, but no killer. Let me explain. The victim is Wolfrid. The weapon is at first glance an innocent-looking ladder and the killer is a hydro-electric dam which is situated fifteen hundred kilometres from here. That doesn't give me a very strong case.'

'Okay, thank you very much, dear gender-neutral colleagues, the inspector has finished,' announced Gerry Gretz.

Naturally, there was a certain amount of protest, but that all ceased immediately when Kolokotronis resumed his traditional implacability.

'Nicely handled,' he said to Gretz. 'I'll see you tonight at the Lesbos and tell you the whole story.'

When Gerry saw Dolorosa again, she was absolutely radiant. He held out the framed, laminated newspaper clipping to her.

'As promised, Mama Dolorosa.'

'Oh I love it when you call me that. My little Pope... I'll just put this away in my treasure chest.'

As she opened the second drawer of her diamond-point pine *armoire*, Gerry caught a glimpse of something sitting right beside Dragana's baby book with its decoration of a long lock of blond hair. What he saw for a quarter of a second was a heap of keys that would have caused the most pompous and domineering of concierges to turn pale with jealousy. But just as he was on the point of asking her about these keys, Mother Milton, who was gifted with second sight, turned to him.

'What keys, Monsieur Gretz?'